SHARE THE MOON

SHARE THE MOON

by
Toni Logan

2021

SHARE THE MOON

ISBN 13: 978-1-63555-844-9

This Trade Paperback Original Is Published By
Bold Strokes Books, Inc.
P.O. Box 249
Valley Falls, NY 12185

First Edition: February 2021

CREDITS
Editor: Barbara Ann Wright
Production Design: Susan Ramundo
Cover Design By Tammy Seidick

Acknowledgments

A heartfelt thank you to Radclyffe, Sandy, and the incredible team at Bold Strokes Books. You've turned a lifelong dream into one of the best rides of my life. I am forever grateful.

To Barbara Ann Wright, editor extraordinaire, for reeling in a head-hopping first draft and putting it on the right track. I am a better writer because of you.

A special shout-out to Tammy Sedick, for capturing the essence of the story and turning it into beautiful cover art.

A huge thank you to my amazing and wonderful friends who joined me on this journey. Especially Jenn, who patiently listened to endless story ideas as I monopolized our dinner conversations.

And finally, the biggest thank you goes to you, the reader, for taking a chance on this book. I hope you enjoy reading it as much as I enjoyed writing it. Cheers.

Dedication

To Mom and Dad. Always loved and forever missed.

Chapter One

1904

"Run!" Lillian's scream echoed in Ruth's head as she sprinted across the open field. Fear surged through her veins as adrenaline propelled her forward. Her heart pounded, and her labored breathing became raspy as she tried to push her body beyond its physical limits. She needed to reach the woods on the far side of the clearing. There she could hide in the shadows of the trees. There she would be safe. But the full moon, that only moments ago had made the perfect romantic backdrop, now betrayed her, like a lantern held high over her head. She was too exposed in its silvery glow, too easy of a target. *Run!* The word continued to bounce around her head as she cursed her stiff new boots. Not a good choice for a quick escape, but running was the last thing she thought she would be doing right now.

She bowed her head and pumped her arms as she willed her body to move faster. *Faster, Ruth, you—*A sharp pain stabbed at her side, causing her upper body to lurch to the left.

She tried to massage away the side stitch. She took a few quick shallow breaths, but a wave of nausea hit her hard. She skidded to a stop, bent forward, and placed her hands on her bent knees. Saliva dripped from her mouth as her stomach began heaving up the meal she'd eaten just moments ago. Ruth gagged and choked with each gut-wrenching spasm. When it was over, she wiped her sleeve across her mouth and took a moment to glance behind her. Two men were on horseback, silhouetted against the moon, galloping full speed in her direction. Rifles held high, they whooped in a battle cry.

"I didn't know," Ruth yelled through gasping breaths. "I didn't know!" She squinted into the night, hoping her words would make the approaching party pause, but they didn't. The men kept coming.

Run! The word welled up inside her, but this time, it was her own voice screaming. A new fear took hold as she started sprinting again. She cleared her mind as much as possible and concentrated on a single tree that marked the entrance to the woods. Make it to that tree, she promised herself, and this nightmare will be over. She pumped her arms twice as fast as before, determination replacing fear. She was going to make it. She was going to be okay. The sound of her short rhythmic breathing echoed in her head and became the cadence her feet responded to. *Come on Ruth, you can do this...you're almost there.* She smiled as the distance between her and the woods diminished. A few more yards and she would be home free, I'm going to make it, she thought as a giddy feeling made her smile.

Then the world spun around her. Ruth's back arched as her upper body twisted to the right, legs stumbling out from under her. She fell hard, facedown, and for a moment, she wondered what had tripped her. But when she tried to get up, searing pain shot through her shoulder, causing her to crumble to the ground. Ruth slowly rolled on her back, cradled her left shoulder, and felt the warm liquid oozing out of the hole in her flesh. She brought her hand close to her face and examined her fingers. She looked quizzically at the bright red blood dripping from them. The thought of actually being shot seemed so implausible.

Run, she heard the voice scream in her head once more, but as the horses galloped upon her, she knew there would be no more running. Ruth flopped her head to the side and focused on the thin legs of the animals dancing around her as they protested the heavy-handed way the men pulled on their reins. *I didn't know*, she tried to announce, but the words never rose above her gurgled breath.

Ruth turned her head back and looked up at the stars. Such a beautiful night, a night that started out with so much hope and promise. "I...didn't...know," she pleaded through gasping breaths as the men sat silent, their agitated horses stomping close to her body.

The sound of a deep whinny mixed with leather creaking as one man leaned over and spit on her. Tears welled in Ruth's eyes as she began to sob. "I didn't know." She coughed.

Her pleas were answered by the click of a rifle being cocked. "No," she cried. "I didn't—" But her next word was drowned out by the sound of a shot ringing in the silent night.

CHAPTER TWO

Present Day

The cool evening was a welcome relief from another muggy, late summer day. Kali Parker rode her 2008 Kawasaki 1400 GTR up the long dirt driveway toward the dilapidated old Victoria house that overlooked a neglected fifty-acre vineyard. She cut the engine at the base of the wraparound porch that was in desperate need of a fresh coat of wood stain, straddled the bike, and waved off the last of the dust that settled around her. She removed her smoky black helmet and placed it on the handlebars as she gently rubbed her fingers through her short hair, coaxing it back into a fashionable messy style. She jabbed the heel of her well-worn brown leather boot at the kickstand, and it obediently sprang forward, allowing her to dismount. She took a moment to brush off a thin layer of dust that clung to her tight, white, V-neck T-shirt and just as tight faded blue jeans.

Kali grabbed her backpack out of the saddlebag and took a moment to admire the full moon sitting low on the horizon.

Beautiful. She smiled as she walked to the front of the house. She took the porch steps two at a time, pulled the squeaky screen door open, and bounded into the house. She used the loud slam to announce her entrance into the main room.

Jamie Carr and Kate Spalding looked up from the overstuffed sage couch that took up a large portion of the spacious vaulted room. Jamie was leaning over the coffee table made of old oak wine barrels, cutting slices off a block of cheddar cheese. Glasses of red wine sat in front of them, and a murder was being solved by the best forensic scientists on the flat screen TV.

"Ladies." Kali let her backpack drop to the floor by the end of the couch, as she glanced at the two most important people in her life. Jamie, her best friend, who had brought her back from the depths of despair after her last breakup, and Kate, the woman who stepped up more than once to fill the void of a motherly role. "Pour me a glass. I just need to get something from my room. Be right back." She bounced up the old wooden staircase.

Her bedroom was at the end of the long narrow hallway, and as she entered the modest-sized room, she back kicked the door with her right boot. The force was not enough to completely close the door, just change its position and provide more privacy. Good enough, she thought as she brought her legs up one at a time, hopping the few short steps to her dresser as she peeled off her boots and socks and let them fall haphazardly on the floor. She pulled out her cell phone and absentmindedly flung it on the dresser. She opened the top left drawer, retrieved a matchbook, and ripped out one of the two remaining paper sticks.

As she closed the cover, she glanced at the logo of the Las Vegas casino resort, and her nipples became hard as a chill raced up her spine. She couldn't remember the woman's name who caused the sudden rush of excitement, but it was clear her body remembered the late-night encounter under the pool's waterfall. *I need to make another trip to Vegas.*

She ran the tip of the match over the strike track and let chemistry do its thing. A romantic glow filled the room as she quickly touched the flame to the wicks of two medium-sized, lavender candles. *What was the name of that woman? Paula? Lisa?* As her mind continued to draw a blank, she replayed the memory of the woman pressed against her back, her hands reached around Kali's chest, caressing her breasts as the water tumbled off the boulders and splashed over them. *Damn, that night was erotic as hell. What was her name?* Kali blew out the match and walked over to her bed. *Oh well, it doesn't matter.*

She sat and reached into the top drawer of her cherry walnut nightstand. She pulled out her wand massager, plugged it in, and flopped on top of the unmade bed. She unzipped her jeans and tugged them down far enough to position the ball of the vibrator comfortably between her legs. She had been horny for the last hour, and she needed release. She took a meditative breath, closed her eyes, and hit the button.

"Buddy! Jeezus!" Kali grunted as an overweight, fifteen-year-old, orange and white tabby cat pounced on the wand. "Go on, get." She shuffled her legs enough to cause the old feline to give up the attack and reposition himself at the foot of her bed. A flick of his tail expressed his annoyance.

"Good boy," Kali whispered, half-irritated and half-amused by the interruption. *Now then, where was I?* She closed her eyes tight and returned the apparatus to the spot that had just begun to satisfy her ache.

A woman in her late twenties appeared on the side of her bed. "Hi, babe. You look gorgeous tonight," Kali said in a hushed breath as she licked her lips.

The woman smiled. "Hi, babe," she whispered. She wore a black dress with a V-neck cut low enough to expose most of her C-cup breasts. Her dark skin was flawless. Her body tight and muscular. She had a thin chiseled face with a slight cleft in her chin, piercing green eyes, and a voice so soft it could still any restless heart. She was stunningly handsome with just the right touch of feminine flare.

Her dark hair parted on the left side and delicately draped over her opposite cheek. "No wait, parted in the middle," Kali requested as the woman ran her fingers through her hair until each piece fell perfectly down the middle. "Better?" she asked.

"Yes," Kali answered, "much sexier. Now I can see both your eyes."

The woman nodded as she repositioned herself on top of Kali. "What do you want me to do to you tonight?"

"You know what I like."

"Yes, I do," she whispered in Kali's ear, causing a chill to tickle down Kali's spine. "You're mine now. Every…single… inch of you."

Kali shivered. "I'm all yours."

The woman's fingers lightly touched Kali's skin as they slowly made their way closer to the vibrator. Another chill caused Kali's nipples to harden. She placed one hand on her breast and squeezed the ache from the tip.

"Those are mine to play with," the woman protested as she placed her hand over Kali's.

"I know they are," Kali said.

The woman smiled that smile that Kali knew so well. That smile that said she knew what Kali was after. That smile that could make Kali come on the spot. That smile that belonged to the only woman who never failed her.

"Right there, baby, keep going. Don't stop…don't… stop." Kali tensed and tightened her thighs as the woman began rubbing a finger around Kali's clitoris, using her wetness to stroke her up and down.

"Go in, baby, please go in. I want to feel you inside me," Kali said out loud as she arched her back and pressed the vibrator more forcefully against her.

"Like this?" More as a statement than a question. She leaned forward over Kali, took her first two fingers and slowly slid them into her. Kali began to thrust into the vibrator. Harder. Faster.

"Don't stop." She bit her lower lip as the words groaned from someplace deep inside. "Oh…baby…don't—"

The dark-haired woman vanished. "What the fuck? Not again." Kali grabbed the end of the vibrator and frantically twisted the cord in an attempt to revive life back into the old toy. It sputtered twice, then nothing. "Shit, not now. Not now."

A slow, acoustic folk melody filled the bedroom as Kali's cell phone came to life. "I know, Jamie…I know." Kali groaned as she glanced at the blinking green glow from her screen that overpowered the dim light from the candles. She knew her vibrator caused the house's electricity to flicker, but right now, she didn't care. She continued to twist the cord as she let the phone ring itself to silence. "Come on old faithful, don't fail me."

The vibrator sputtered and teased before finally roaring back to life. *Finally!* Kali took a moment to take another deep meditative breath and closed her eyes, hoping the mood was not ruined. "Ah, there you are."

The beautiful, dark-haired woman appeared from a dense fog. "Miss me?"

"You know I did, now finish me. I'm so close."

"You know I always do," whispered the woman as she pressed her muscular body onto Kali's. She kissed Kali in a hard, possessive way, then slowly let her fingers glide down Kali's body until they were once again covered in wetness. "I'll be back," the woman whispered as she licked her way down until her tongue and fingers became one.

"Damn it, Kali," Jamie mumbled to her cell phone as it floated to voice mail. "She needs to find herself a girlfriend before I kill her." She tossed the phone back on the coffee table, tugged at the dark blue cotton T-shirt that clung to her, and pressed into the cushion of the couch as she pouted. She glanced at the flickering TV screen and sighed. Frustrated, she blew at a strand of her hair as it tickled its way across her face. All she could do now was wait.

From the opposite end of the large, C-shaped couch, Kate looked over and smiled. She uncrossed her ankles and slid them off the coffee table as she leaned forward. She grabbed the bottle of Merlot and topped off the half-empty glass that sat in front of Jamie. "In my opinion, both of you need to find yourselves a girlfriend."

"I'm over women," Jamie insisted as she grabbed her glass.

"You know, they're not all assholes."

"I know." Jamie sighed. *I'm just ass-holed out.* And tired of giving so much of herself to women who didn't think twice about throwing her under a bus when the relationship got a little rocky. Why were some women so painfully addictive? She shook the thoughts away as she took a gulp, closed her eyes, and welcomed the perfect blend of smooth and oaky semi-sweetness. *Damn, that's good.* She smiled as she opened her eyes and glanced at Kate.

Kate, the surviving lover of Jamie's Aunt Nora, was a sixty-eight-year-old hippie who looked and dressed as if she was still living in the 1970s. She was tall and lean and had long, gray-streaked hair that was always pulled back in a tight ponytail, exposing a face that had a gentle glow and light brown eyes that sparkled with kindness. Jamie was sure each wrinkled line on her tan and weathered face was the beginning sentence to an amazing story. Kate was well traveled, held certificates in Viticulture and Enology, and never seemed to have a bad day. *If only you were younger.* Jamie coughed loudly as she choked. *Oh my God, I can't believe I just thought that.* She leaned forward and placed her wineglass back on the coffee table.

"You okay?"

"Um…yeah…just went down the wrong way." She made a fist and thumped on her chest as she coughed twice more. She waved her hand in front of her face in an attempt to clear the thoughts away. *Ew, that was a bit incestuous.*

"And…we're back." Kate nodded at the TV as it returned to normal.

"That was—"

The sound of Kali bounding down the stairs made Jamie look over her shoulder. Buddy was in the lead, his sagging stomach swaying as he waddled down each step. He slipped a bit when he hit the hardwood floor but quickly regained his footing. Seconds later, he was on top of the coffee table checking out the food. "Oh no, you don't." Kate grabbed him and a slice of cheese and put both on the floor. "There you go, sweetie."

Kali walked to the couch, threw her legs over the back, and rode the cushion down to the seat. She snatched the empty glass waiting for her, grabbed the bottle, and poured.

Kate started clapping slowly. "I'm impressed. Record time tonight."

"Seriously?" Jamie frowned. "You're encouraging this?" She turned to Kali. "The next time you feel the need to get off,

could you please check with us first? You know the wiring in
this house is worse since the last storm, and every time you use
your vibrator, it messes with the TV."

"Or at least wait until a commercial break." Kate winked.

"Maybe it wasn't me. Maybe Charlie's messing with the
TV." Kali chuckled as she downed her glass in three gulps and
poured another.

"Nah, Charlie just haunts the vineyard. Never seen him
lurking around the house." Kate tossed a folded cheese slice to
Buddy, who batted it around a few times before devouring it.

"See?" Jamie pointed to Kali. "Don't be putting this on
Charlie."

Kali laughed as she stuffed a thick slice of cheese between
two crackers and shoved the entire thing in her mouth.

Charlie was the name given to the resident ghost of the
vineyard who, according to family rumor, was a young horse
thief who received justice at the end of Great Grandpa Hank's
rifle. At first, the ghostly sightings had only happened during
a full moon. On those evenings, Hank had drunk himself into
a stupor, had stood on the front porch, and had yelled, "We
didn't know," into the night.

As the months passed, the sightings had increased and so
had Hank's drinking, until one night, he'd downed a bottle
of whiskey and had never woken up. The land had passed to
Jamie's Grandpa Fred and eventually to her dad and his sister,
Nora. By then, the rundown house and overgrown land were
in dire need of attention. But where Jamie's dad had seen hard
work, a waste of money, and "too much trouble," Aunt Nora had

seen endless possibilities and magic. In the end, they'd agreed Nora would be the sole recipient of the land, and Jamie's dad had received all other family possessions, including stocks, an antique automobile, and a sizable bank account.

By then, sightings of the boyish figure had become daily occurrences around the vineyard. Most days, Charlie could be seen walking, keeping to himself, and doing nothing in particular. Nora tried on multiple occasions to approach him, but he would disappear before she even got close. Her brother had suggested they hire a ghost hunter, a medium, or perform a séance to try and rid the land of him, but Nora wouldn't hear of it. She thought having a spirit on the land was a good omen, and as such, should be left alone.

Eventually, Nora named the ghost Charlie and said anyone who had been hanging around the land for that long was like family and needed a proper name. Jamie's father thought she was nuts, and when they came to visit Nora, forbade Jamie to go anywhere near Charlie, especially if they happened to be visiting the vineyard during a full moon. On those evenings, he would sit at the far southeast corner of the land, arms wrapped around his bent knees, rocking back and forth. Nora didn't know why the moon seemed to bring out this unusual behavior. Charlie was a ghost; ghosts, like everyone else, apparently did weird things.

Jamie had learned she and Kate were next in line to inherit Charlie, along with the vineyard, last year when Aunt Nora had been on her deathbed. "The place belongs to you and my beloved Kate now," Aunt Nora had weakly whispered. "Get out of that damn job you hate so much and come enjoy the land. Kate and I have had the best years of our lives there."

Jamie had squeezed her aunt's hand, "I know you have."

"And don't you even think about selling it."

"I won't, Aunt Nora."

"And don't let anyone mess with Charlie. He has a right to exist in peace."

When Jamie was a child, her aunt would talk about the wonders of the world and how she thought most people were ignorant assholes for not believing in the possibilities of the unknown. Nora had thought Jamie's father fit into that category, and his views on ghosts and the paranormal were a combination of horseshit and arrogance. The only reason Charlie creeped him out so much, Nora said, was because he was scared he would get stuck as a ghost and have to live his pathetic little life over and over again.

"The vineyard is a magical place, Jamie, who knows, maybe it's where you'll finally find what you've always been looking for."

A cracker flew with skilled accuracy across the couch and beamed Jamie in the middle of her forehead as Nora's words faded from her mind. "Ouch, Kali." She rubbed the spot where the cracker hit.

"Have you been into Kate's pot?" Kali sat deep into the cushion, arms folded across her chest in an accusatory posture.

"What? No, why would you say that?"

"You were totally spacing out as I was talking. If you're not stoned, then let's hope this isn't some early onset thing you've got going on."

Jamie threw a slice of cheese at her. "I was thinking about Aunt Nora."

"Am I going to have to separate the two of you?" Kate said.

"She started it." Jamie pointed to Kali, who promptly stuck out her tongue. Jamie giggled as she reached for her glass of wine. Memories of the endless nights she'd spent sobbing in Kali's arms after Nora had passed danced in her head. *You are my rock, my friend, and I can't imagine my world without you.* "Anyway, what were you saying?"

"I have a meeting tomorrow morning at Legacy Lesbians. I'm going to talk about adding the vineyard to their website. Under venues that host weddings and receptions."

Jamie was speechless and impressed. When Kali had first mentioned she wanted to expand the reach of the vineyard to weddings, Jamie wasn't convinced she could pull it off. If Kali could actually get Legacy Lesbians to sponsor them, that would be a huge win for the vineyard.

Legacy was the brainchild of two ex-lovers who'd started sponsoring lesbian-themed events around the west coast but predominately in California. They eventually teamed up with several B-level corporations and semi-well-known lesbian celebrities. As their success grew, so did their reach, which now included a variety of luxurious travel trips and all things wedding.

Jamie nibbled on some cheese. "Kali, that's fantastic. How did you manage that?"

"I may or may not have once slept with Paige, the woman who was just hired to handle their west coast marketing."

"I'll put money down on the 'may have' option. And this is awesome, I must say. I'm really impressed. Getting exposure on their website could really help elevate the status of the vineyard from life support to just critical." Jamie had promised her aunt she would take care of the vineyard for her. She knew what the land had meant to Nora, and she also knew if she lost it on her watch, she would never forgive herself.

"Hey, don't write this place off. It still produces a damn good product," Kate said as she shook her finger at Jamie.

"That it does," Jamie stood and arched her back to stretch. She was tired and sore from working all day on an irrigation leakage in the north field. They needed to replace several of the lines due to leaks in the tubing, but for right now, all they could afford to do was patch it with tape. *Why does it feel like everything about this house and vineyard is being held together with duct tape and a prayer?* "And on that note, I think I'm going to take my ass and my glass outside and enjoy the beautiful evening." Jamie grabbed the wine and topped off her glass. "Anyone want some more?" Kali and Kate both shook their heads. "All right then." She looked around. "Anyone see the cork?"

"Buddy!" Kate pointed to what was left of a completely chewed cork next to slobbery pieces of half-eaten cheese.

"I've got this." Kali jumped up and motioned for the bottle. She walked over to her backpack, pulled out a tampon, and pushed the extra absorbent end in the neck of the bottle.

Jamie scrunched her face in disgust. "Okay, wow, now I'll never be able to un-see that."

"What? It makes the perfect cork. And see?" Kali grabbed the string. "It even comes with a built-in uncorking device."

"That's disgusting." Jamie rolled her eyes as she walked toward the screen door. "I'll be on the porch if anyone needs me."

"Enjoy." Kate half-heartedly waved as she reached for another slice of cheese.

The screen door squeaked in rusty protest as Jamie pushed it open. *Is there anything in this house that doesn't need fixing?* It was a daunting thought, and it weighed heavy on her at times. In the last few years, care for the vineyard had come in a distant second to the care of her Aunt Nora's deteriorating health. If it were not for Kate tirelessly tending to both, Jamie feared the place would have gone under by now. What money the vineyard currently brought in barely covered expenses. What was left was being funneled back into the land. Repairs on the house weren't going to happen in the foreseeable future. *Why did I leave a steady and predictable job for this?*

"Because you've felt more alive the past seven months than the last thirty-two years," Jamie said as she shuffled to an old wooden bench, a souvenir from one of the many trips Nora had made south of the border. Jamie plopped down, leaned back, and stared at the full moon. She took a sip of wine, sighed, and for the first time in a long time, thought about Cheryl.

They had been together five years and had been separated over three. *What a waste.* Jamie exhaled as she took another sip. Cheryl was a struggling musician, well-liked in her circle of friends. They'd met at a New Year's Eve party thrown by a mutual acquaintance, and by the time the ball had dropped, their fate had been sealed. Promises of *forever* and *you're the one* had been exchanged within the first month. The U-Haul had come in the third month, and by the end of the sixth, they had merged every aspect of their lives, and Jamie had never felt more settled. With Cheryl, Jamie had hoped to finally create the home life she'd never had growing up. One that was lasting and predictable.

The first signs of trouble had been apparent early on. What had started out as backhanded comments by Cheryl soon morphed into sarcastic criticism and eventually, flat-out verbal abuse. Apologetic "It won't happen again," "I was stressed out," and "you took my words out of context," became common as months turned into years. When the apologies and flowers had stopped coming, and Cheryl's mysterious unaccounted blocks of time had become the norm, Jamie had had enough. Her world was unraveling, and it was taking her down with it. The stable life she had so desperately sought had alluded her once again. *The never-ending story of my life.*

Never again, Jamie promised for the millionth time as she took a gulp and looked over the land. *Why are relationships so difficult?* She leaned her head back against the wall and closed her eyes. The slight cool breeze felt wonderful. "Never again," she repeated as she finished her glass, placed it on the floor, and allowed the fatigue of another long day carry her into a peaceful sleep.

"I know you're not reading because the TV's messing up again." Kate's loud words traveled onto the porch, waking Jamie. *Kali really needs to find herself a girlfriend.* Jamie chuckled as she yawned and slowly opened her eyes.

"Holy shit!" Her foot caught on the bench as she jumped up, and she fell hard. Her heart was racing, and a moment of fear gripped her as she tried to focus. "Charlie?" Jamie cocked her head at the familiar figure sitting on the bench, smiling.

"Well, actually...my name's Ruth."

Not a teenage boy but a woman. Jamie took a moment to scan her. She was dressed in the same outfit Jamie had always seen her in; gray tweed pants, black suspenders, white collared shirt, and boots. Up until this moment, Jamie had assumed like everyone else that their vineyard ghost was a teenage boy. An easy assumption to make, based on Ruth's short hair and men's attire, but up close, Jamie could clearly see the woman under the guise. And it caused a flutter in her stomach that she hadn't felt in years.

Jamie stared at Ruth's flawless, life-like complexion, the choppy way her short dark hair was layered, as though she had cut it herself, an ear to ear smile that was both shy and confident... and those eyes. Those beautiful, sparkling, crystal gray eyes that held Jamie in a trance. Ruth looked so...real, so...alive, so gorgeous. The fact that she was a ghost was momentarily forgotten as Jamie's nipples hardened in response to the woman in front of her, who was looking as alive as she was.

"I'm sorry I startled you and um..." Ruth gestured to an area on her forehead. "You have something right here."

It took a moment for Jamie to register what Ruth was saying, as though her words were floating in the air, just out of reach. "Oh, I…" When Jamie's brain finally arranged the words in an understandable sentence, she gently scrubbed a cracker crumb from her forehead. "Thanks…wait." She tilted her head. "How is it that I'm hearing you?"

"I don't understand what you mean."

"I hear you talking."

"I hear you talking too."

"Yeah, but you're a—"

The rusty squeak of the screen door startled her. She looked over her shoulder as Kate peeked out from behind the door. "Girl, what the hell you doing on the floor?"

"Talking to…" Jamie gestured toward the bench, but Ruth had vanished, along with the butterflies that had been fluttering around her stomach. "Um, huh, I…" There was a part of Jamie that wanted to jump up and share the excitement of the interaction, but she hesitated. There was something that felt intimate about the exchange. Something that for now, she wanted to keep private. She needed to sit and analyze the emotions that were still lingering within her. Emotions she didn't want to let go of. "Never mind," she mumbled, lost in thought as she stared at the bench.

"You sure you haven't been in my stash?" Kate raised an eyebrow as she stepped onto the porch.

"No, Kate, I haven't been into your pot. I tripped getting up off the bench, that's all." She cocked her head, "Why, what's up?"

"Kali's upstairs messing with herself again, and it ruined the big reveal of who the killer was in the show. I swear, that girl's not normal. Anyway, I figured while she's up there doing her thing, I'd come out and sit with you if that's okay?" Kate frowned. "But I ain't sitting on the floor."

Jamie waved Kate over and motioned for help up. Kate heaved her up, and the two of them shuffled to the bench. Jamie froze as Kate sat in the exact spot that Ruth had been sitting in just moments ago. The fluttering in Jamie's stomach returned.

"What's the matter, did I sit in pigeon shit again?" Kate cocked her left hip as she lifted enough to crane her neck.

"What? Oh no, no," Jamie said as she sat next to her. "You didn't sit in anything."

"Well, then, stop acting weird." Kate wrapped an arm around her, and Jamie rested her head on Kate's shoulder. "Beautiful night, huh?"

Jamie nodded. "Kate?"

"Hmm?"

"Do you ever wonder about the afterlife?"

"All the time since Nora died, why?"

"Wouldn't it be nice to know that after we die, we really can communicate with our loved ones again?"

"Hell, I communicate with Nora every day, and I'd like to think in her own way, she's talking back. In fact, yesterday I noticed the glass pie dish she always cooked in was cracked. I figured that was her way of letting me know she was pissed because I changed her favorite recipe. I always told her she used too much butter and not enough cinnamon in her apple pie."

Jamie smiled as she thought of the many days she'd sat with Kate and Nora, eating pie and laughing. Wouldn't it be nice to have the chance to talk to Nora one more time, like she did with Ruth?

"I hope this place makes it." Jamie stared into the darkness of the vineyard as an image of Ruth flashed in her head.

Kate patted her shoulder. "It will darlin…it's made it this far."

CHAPTER THREE

Jamie bobbed her head and tapped her hands on the steering wheel of a rusty all-terrain golf cart as she mouthed the lyrics to one of her favorite songs blaring from her Bluetooth earbuds. She welcomed the warmth of the morning sun on her skin as she slowly made her way up a narrow row of Cabernet Sauvignon grapes. Her thoughts quickly drifted to her encounter with Ruth.

Damn, she was beautiful, Jamie thought as her body reacted. It was times like this that Jamie felt the sting of being alone. Strike that, not alone. She had Kali and Kate and a handful of amazing friends, and she had a business that brought her back to her love of nature. Alone was definitely the wrong word.

"Single." Jamie whispered the word that she had learned to embrace, as though it was something to be ashamed of. A scarlet letter of sorts. "Single by choice," she reminded herself, then quietly repeated her promise. "Never again." If being single the rest of her life meant never having to deal with the heartache of watching her girlfriend fall in love with another woman, then sign her up.

She stopped the cart halfway down the row, removed her earbuds, and gently slid them in the front pocket of her jeans. She took a moment to admire the fruit that hung in clusters from vines that were starting their magical turn from hard green grapes to plump purple clusters. In a few weeks, they would be ready to harvest. If the sugar, acid, and tannin levels were good, this crop could put them in the black. Wouldn't that be nice, Jamie thought as she tried to push the alternative out of her mind. Lately, they had been getting offers from developers to buy the land at top market value, but the thought of the vines being bulldozed to make way for buildings and parking lots made her sick.

Jamie turned off the cart, grabbed a shovel from the back, and started digging. The soil had a soft sandy texture that was easy to penetrate. Two shovels later, Jamie nodded. "That should do." She leaned into the back of the golf cart and grabbed Kali's vibrator by the cord. She held it for a ceremonious moment as it swayed in the slight morning breeze. "Sorry, old girl," she said as she opened her fingers and let the device drop into the hole. *Mother Nature, if you're a lesbian, please accept this gift.* She smiled at the thought as she scooped the fresh mound of dirt back into the small pit. Moments later, as she patted it down, a long shadow slid over her.

Kate sat bareback on Ginger, her mellow, twenty-two-year-old, sorrel quarter horse that she'd rescued from a rancher who rode her so hard, he blew out her front legs. First thing every morning, Kate took Ginger on an easy stroll around the property as part of her recovery therapy, a ritual that Kate enjoyed as much as she hoped Ginger did. "I take it Kali doesn't know about this?"

"Nope." Jamie jabbed the shovel into the ground and leaned against the handle.

"Uh-huh." Kate paused. "You know you're going to catch a boatload of shit for doing that."

"Yeah, I know, but I plan on buying her a battery operated one later today when I go into the city. I'm hoping she'll forgive me if I get her one with all the latest attachments and speed levels."

"Uh-huh," Kate repeated. "Think I'll be out of the house when Kali comes home this afternoon. In case there's any flying debris."

Jamie laughed. "Maybe I should wear my bike helmet around the house for the next couple of days."

"Wouldn't hurt," Kate said as Jamie gently stroked Ginger above her nose. The horse responded by lowering her head and nestling into Jamie's chest. Kate had worked wonders with Ginger. She never pushed the old mare beyond her comfort zone or abilities, and in the end, Ginger's love and affection came pouring out. Kate was good that way; she always put the feelings of others first, and thought all beings were her equal. "Hey, Kate?" Jamie glanced into the eyes of the kindest woman she had ever known.

"Hmm?"

"Of all the times you've seen Charlie hanging around, did you ever"—Jamie gestured by bobbing her head sideways—"um...you know?"

"Don't suppose you could throw a few more words out? You know, those pesky little things that when strung together make a complete sentence?"

"Did you ever, you know, speak to her?"

"Her?" Kate cocked her head.

"Charlie isn't a he...he's a she. Her name's Ruth." She glanced down as she said the name, aware that she was smiling like a school kid with a crush.

"A woman. Well I'll be damned."

"I know, right?"

"Huh, so that means—"

"It was probably Ruth who was murdered on this land and not a teenage boy." A protective feeling surged through her body at the thought of anyone hurting Ruth. A feeling that surprised her. She had seen Ruth on the land since she was a toddler and had never before felt such a strong emotional pull. Jamie chuckled to herself at the thought of protecting a ghost. *A little late in the game for that.*

"A woman," Kate repeated as she drifted into silent thought.

"I kinda talked to her last night, on the porch before you came out." Jamie smiled as she replayed the memory for the umpteenth time.

"While you were on the floor?"

"What? No, not while I was on the floor. Well, I mean, yes, I was on the floor, but she was on the bench."

"Why weren't you on the bench?"

"Because she scared me, and I fell off. What does that even matter? What matters is we spoke. As in talked." Jamie scolded herself for snapping.

"I understand the definition of the word."

Jamie closed her eyes and let out a long sigh that tingled throughout her body as she exhaled the words. "She has a beautiful voice...and face."

Kate sat a little taller. "Sorry I interrupted the party."

"What? No! She's a ghost. I mean, how creepy is that, right?" The thought of kissing Ruth's lips flashed in her head. Would they be as soft as they looked? Or would they be...*oh my God Jamie, get a grip.* Ruth was a ghost, as in back from the dead. Kissing her, no matter how kissable her lips looked, was still kissing a deceased person. *Ew.*

Kate gently stroked Ginger's neck as she smiled. "If you say so."

"What does that mean?"

"Nothing. Did she say what happened to her?"

"No, we didn't get that far in our conversation." She thought back to the family rumor and dismissed the thought of Ruth stealing her great grandfather's horse. There was something about Ruth that looked too innocent and kind to steal anything from anyone. There had to be another explanation as to why a woman in her prime ended up dead on their land.

"Well, how far did you get?"

"She told me I had a cracker crumb on my forehead and that her name was Ruth," Jamie said as her cheeks flushed.

Kate threw her head back and laughed.

"Isn't this freaking you out, even the slightest?" Jamie was taken aback by Kate's comfortable reaction. Or was she taken aback by the fact that the only woman who had stirred her desire in over three years was a ghost? She had been on a handful of dates since her breakup with Cheryl but declined when several asked her out a second time. It wasn't that they weren't nice women, all of them were; it was more that none of them woke the butterflies in her stomach like Ruth did.

"Honey, this is California. I've seen some weird ass shit in my time that makes Char…I mean Ruth, walking around the vineyard child's play. 'Bout time an introduction was made." Kate paused. "You know, your aunt tried to approach her on several occasions, but every time she got close, Ruth would disappear. One time, Nora actually left a bowl of food out for her. I told her Ruth wasn't a stray dog that needed feeding. She was a ghost, and ghosts don't eat. But don't you know, that entire bowl of fruit was gone the next morning. Shows you what I know."

Jamie stood silent and stared, focusing on Kate's mouth moving but not comprehending a word she was saying. After an awkward moment of silence, Kate leaned down and snapped a finger in front of Jamie's face. "You doing okay in that brain of yours?"

"I talked to a ghost, Kate. A ghost. And not only that, she was beautiful. I skipped right over the insanity of having a conversation with a dead person and went right for the attraction. I actually had a physical reaction to a nonphysical person. So, no, right now, I'm not doing so well in this brain of mine."

"Jamie, you've known Ruth, since you were a child. She's familiar to you."

"Don't try to normalize this Kate. Everything about this is certifiable, and you know it. Why do you think my family never mentioned Ruth outside of our inner circle? And even then, it was in hushed tones." The exact tone they'd used when talking about Jamie's sexual preference after she came out to them. As though Jamie had chosen a lifestyle that would embarrass them and possibly bring gossip. Jamie learned a long time ago that her parent's hush tones were code for anything they deemed "unacceptable."

"Your family talked about your aunt and I in hushed tones, so I wouldn't use that as a measuring stick." Before Jamie could fire off another hyperventilated response, Kate continued. "And I'm not discounting what you're feeling. And yes, on the surface, being attracted to a ghost is kinda out there, but I've known Ruth as long as I've lived here. Though I will admit, when Nora first pointed her out, I was a little freaked. But as time passed, seeing her around just felt normal."

Sadness washed over Jamie as she thought about the decades Ruth had been on this land. No one had ever seen another ghost on the vineyard, and Jamie wondered if Ruth ever felt lonely.

"Several years ago," Kate continued, "Nora noticed Ruth was starting to come around more and more when we would take our morning walks. She would say, 'Don't look, but I think Charlie's following us.' And sure enough, there she'd be, strolling along a distance behind us. Nora got to the point where she could sense when Ruth was close by. Your aunt always viewed her presence on this land as a sign that this place was magical in some way. That's why we left the southeast corner of the property alone. That part of the land seemed to mean something to her, and Nora didn't feel right messing with it."

Jamie inhaled a quick breath, but before she exhaled a single word, Kate held her finger up to indicate she wasn't done. "I wouldn't overanalyze this. We all know where this would land you on most people's radar. But I don't really give a shit what people think, and you know what, Jamie, there's a wonderful freedom in that. So my advice…just go with it. I don't claim to know anything about ghosts, but there has to be some reason she's still sticking around. If she approached you, maybe something's up. Hell, Nora sure tried her damnedest to win her over."

Jamie let out a sigh and remained silent. Why did Ruth approach her? After all these years, why now, and why her?

Ginger started pawing the ground. "Well, anyway, we better get a move on. Ginger needs to get her walking time in." Kate nudged the horse forward. "When you gonna see her next?"

"We, uh, I don't know."

"Well, invite her over for dinner one night to hang out with us, but wait until Kali calms down. Wouldn't want to scare her off. Speaking of, text me when it's safe."

"Coward."

Kate gave Jamie a backhanded wave as Ginger slowly plodded down the row. Jamie loved Kate as much as she had her aunt. They had both been there for her when she'd needed a hand to crawl out of the rabbit hole that had consumed her life so many years ago. A dark and deep place, where Jamie had thought the only way out was suicide. She had been falling apart at the seams, and no one had seemed to notice. Had it not been for that fateful moment when Kate and Nora had walked into the coffee shop on the night she was closing up, Jamie feared the chapters that now made up her book of life would look drastically different. I don't know what I would have done without the two of you, Jamie thought as echoes of her aunt's voice danced in her head.

"I met Kate," Nora had told Jamie, "at a women's music festival held on a private ranch in the upper regions of Northern California. Those were the days where we could all walk around topless, with nothing on but cutoff jeans and flip flops, which made it hard having a conversation with attractive women, if you know what I mean." Nora would say as she cackled her signature, high-pitched laugh. "On the last night of the festival, I was stretched out on a blanket with a few friends, drinking wine and listening to the music when Kate came walking by. Damn, that girl could rock a pair of cutoffs. She was goddamned beautiful, and when she turned and smiled at me, I knew she was the one I wanted to be with. We stayed up all night, smoking pot and talking. She told me she worked for one of the wineries in the area, and how she hated the patriarchal dominance of the business. That's when I told her about my land and how I always dreamed of someday turning it into a vineyard."

By the end of that week, Kate was on Nora's land, taking soil samples, and one month later, she'd moved into the old Victorian house as a permanent resident. "She talked me into investing in organic grapes, you know. Said there would be a huge market for organic wine, and she was right. She's always right. It's her gift. Mine's dancing." Nora had jumped up and started swaying her hips and waving her arms in the air. "Can't get through life without dancing."

Kate and Nora had worked the land from sunrise to sunset, seven days a week, until their first sizable crop had been ready to harvest. Kate had brought samples of their grapes over to Chanadoah, a winery about twenty minutes down the road. It was a family-owned business, and Kate had just happened to be close friends with Mick, the family's oldest son. Chanadoah Winery had quickly set Nora's vineyard up as one of their suppliers for an organic wine they had been producing on the side. "It didn't make me wealthy, but you can never put a price on a labor of love," Nora would always say, then add, "and besides, I found my soulmate in the journey."

"You sure did," Jamie smiled as Nora's voice and image faded away and was replaced by the birds chirping in the vineyard. She blinked in her reality as a warmth filled her heart. *What I wouldn't give to be able to see you again.* She grabbed the shovel and threw it into the back of her all-terrain golf cart.

"Hi."

Jamie jumped as she slapped her hand across her chest. "Jeezus!"

"Sorry, I seem to keep startling you." Ruth sat in the golf cart, swinging her legs out and back, making *thump-thump* sounds as the boots hit the metal.

"Maybe we can come up with a warning signal before you just…materialize. Or maybe you could just walk up to me like normal." Jamie glanced at Ruth, and her stomach flutters returned.

"So." Ruth cleared her throat. "What were you burying?"

"You saw that, huh?"

"I see pretty much everything that goes on around here."

"Great." Jamie's stomach bottomed out as all the personal things she had done in private around the house danced in her mind. "Ever been in the house?"

"No."

"Can't or just haven't?"

"Haven't. I never wanted to intrude."

"Well, maybe that's a good thing."

"So what were you burying?" Ruth curiously repeated.

"It was a…uh…it wasn't mine."

"If it wasn't yours, why are you burying it?" Ruth smiled that beautiful, ear to ear smile that Jamie found so enticing, so beautiful, so…kissable. *Oh my God, has it been that long since I've had sex, that my body is still reacting to Ruth? And just when I canceled therapy because I was starting to feel normal again after Cheryl.* "Um." Jamie shook off the thought. "It's a long story involving electrical surges both in the house and in Kali."

Ruth cocked her head. "I don't understand."

"It's probably best you don't…so um." Jamie reached out. "My name's—"

"Jamie, yes, I know I've watched you grow up. You were such a cute kid. Always getting into trouble and stuff."

"Well, I'm sure not always." Jamie sorted as she lightheartedly defended herself, knowing perfectly well that Ruth had watched her go through life's cringeworthy young-and-dumb phase.

Ruth nodded. "Yeah, pretty much always, from what I saw." Ruth reached toward Jamie's extended hand, and as her fingers closed around Jamie's, a flash of energy hit her chest as a clear and vivid memory surged through her mind. She was darting in and out of overgrown vines, and their leaves tickled across her face. She heard herself giggle as someone clamped onto her waist and hoisted her high in the air. She remembered the sunshine on her face and a slight breeze across her body.

"I told you I'd find you," Ruth had lowered Jamie to the ground and scrubbed her fingers through Jamie's hair.

"Again," Jamie had pleaded.

"Okay little princess, one more time. Now go hide."

Jamie jerked away from Ruth, took a couple of quick breaths, and asked, "Did we…did we play—"

"Hide and seek? Yes, when your parents were fighting, you would wander off unattended. I thought the best way to keep an eye on you and make sure you were safe was to engage you in a game. I would jump out from behind the vines, and you would squeal, 'Found you.'"

"Wait...you would jump out at me?" Jamie closed her eyes, and saw a memory of Ruth hopping out from behind a vine, arms extended, ready to tickle at any moment.

"Yes, moments after you opened your eyes from counting to five."

"Doesn't that kind of go against the definition of the 'hide' part of the game?" Jamie smiled at Ruth as the joy that she had felt so long ago returned. *I remember.*

"Well, when we first started playing, you would cry after a few seconds if you couldn't find me, so I kind of changed the rules."

"Wow, after all these years, I feel so betrayed to learn this." Jamie playfully placed her hand over her chest.

Ruth smiled. "You enjoyed the game so much, you started to run away from your parents when they weren't looking and come find me. You would have your arms out, and I would scoop you up and twirl you around. Then you would tell me to hide. I would put you down, jump behind the vine, and when you counted to five, I'd jump back out." Ruth paused as she gazed at Jamie. "And look at you now."

Jamie saw Ruth's eyes rake over her body, and it made her smile. *Could the attraction be mutual?* "So why did we stop interacting? I don't remember."

"Your parents stopped bringing you around, and when you did finally return, you were older. A teenager, and I could sense you had changed. You seemed so—"

"Dark...out of it...antisocial? Yeah, that time of my life wasn't the best representation of myself." Jamie frowned as she looked down. They had been the worst years of her life. The spillover from the toxic relationship between her parents had made her angry and withdrawn. Depression had set in, her grades had tanked, and she'd lost her sense of self. Her world became a black hole, and she didn't know how to crawl out. "I do remember that when I was a kid, my dad and Aunt Nora would get into fights, and then they just stopped speaking to each other. My dad forbade me to ever see or talk to her again, and to this day, I never knew why."

"Your father was pressuring Nora to sell the property."

"What? Why would he do that?" The words were like a punch to her gut. Nora had loved this land; everyone in the family knew that. Why would her father think Nora would agree to sell the one thing that meant as much to her as Kate?

"He was approached by someone who wanted to buy the land after Kate and Nora turned it into a vineyard. Your father stood to make a lot from commission on the deal if he could convince Nora to cash out. It was during the time your parents were divorcing, and he needed the money."

"How do you know all this, and I don't?"

"Nora and Kate would take long walks around the land and talk about it. I would overhear. It was a very upsetting time for them and me. I didn't want her to sell the land and leave. I really liked Nora. They took extra steps to acknowledge and make me feel welcome."

"Neither Kate or Aunt Nora ever told me this. When I asked what happened, they said a fight got out of hand between Nora and my dad, and things went very wrong."

"They never wanted to taint your feelings about your parents, especially your father."

Jamie remembered the constant fighting and tension between her parents in the years of pre- and post-divorce. Jamie's mom had accused her dad of losing their savings in a series of bad investments that she didn't know about and definitely didn't agree to. Endless arguments eventually turned into a nasty divorce and heated custody battle, putting Jamie in the middle of her parents "he said, she said" mudslinging accusations. No wonder she'd felt suicidal at such a young age. She had figured the only way to stop the madness that had become her life was to no longer be a participant. And besides, she'd reasoned, who would miss her. *No one.*

"Dad had to know Nora would never sell the land. She loved this place. It's the only thing she asked for after Grandpa Fred died."

Ruth nodded. "Nora brought that up several times to your father when he came around demanding she sell." Ruth frowned. "Those conversations always ended in a bad fight. I think deep down, Nora loved your dad but…"

"She loved the land more."

"Yes, she did, and she wasn't about to just let it go. That's why she decided to give it to you and Kate upon her death. She knew neither of you would sell out."

A sadness fell over Jamie as she thought about the crappy apartment she and her mom had moved into because her parents had needed to sell their home to pay off the mounting debt. The endless nights she'd cried herself to sleep, the anger she'd felt when there was no extra money to be spent on her childhood wants and desires, even with her mom working two jobs. The never-ending jabs she'd endured from her classmates as it became harder and harder to fit in at school when she felt as if her world was crashing in around her. It was no wonder Jamie had become reclusive and anti-social. Better to stay in the shadows of life. At least there, the darkness could hide the truth. There, she didn't feel like such an outcast. She wished she could have just fit in and been normal like the other kids. *But there was nothing about my home life that was normal.*

When Jamie turned sixteen, her mom had insisted she stop moping around the apartment and get a job. It had been a nonnegotiable request and one that had struck fear in Jamie. A job meant she would have to interact with people. She would have rather stuck a fork in her eye. But to get her mom off her back, Jamie had reluctantly filled out an application at a coffee house a mile from their apartment and around the corner from her high school. She'd prayed every night that she would not be hired. But her prayers had gone unanswered, and two weeks later, Jamie had entered the working world as a part-time barista. She'd hated the job, she'd hated her mom, and more than ever, she'd hated life. *Funny how that dumb little job played such a big role in changing my life.*

Jamie had requested to work the evening shift, and once there, she would always strike the same deal with her fellow coworkers. She would clean the place while they took drink orders from people who spent more on their caffeine addiction then Jamie spent on a full day's meals. A deal her coworkers had happily agreed to, and one that had taken Jamie out of direct contact with the public.

One evening, as Jamie was about to lock up, Kate and Nora had come strolling in. Jamie hadn't realized how much she'd missed them until she'd run over and buried herself deep within their welcoming arms. Tears had poured down her cheeks as she'd sobbed. That single embrace had unlocked emotions Jamie had kept away in the shadows since she was a young girl.

It didn't take long before they'd come up with a plan. First, they'd all agreed Jamie should not tell her mom or dad that Kate and Nora were back in her life. Second, Jamie would lay the groundwork and inform her mom that she'd made a new friend at work and that she was going to start doing things with her after school. Third, Jamie would then text Nora and Kate, and they'd come pick her up and take her to the vineyard. A plan that Jamie credited with saving her life because time spent with Nora and Kate always left her feeling welcome, loved, and well-fed. The vineyard had soon become Jamie's sanctuary and eventually a hideaway to bring her girlfriends since her mom not only refused to accept her sexual preference, she had flat out forbidden it. With Nora and Kate back in Jamie's life, her depression had lifted, and for the first time in a long time, Jamie had started loving life again.

She smiled as the memories flooded her head. She turned to share some stories about her time with Nora and Kate with Ruth but paused as she realized the life this land had breathed back into her soul was just the opposite for Ruth.

Sorrow filled Jamie's heart. "Ruth, what happened to you? My whole life, I heard a story about a teenage boy being murdered because he tried to steal a horse from my great-grandpa. That was you, wasn't it?"

Ruth turned and stared at the far southeast corner of the land. The same place Jamie had seen her on so many full moon nights. "I didn't know," Ruth choked out as she turned and locked eyes with Jamie.

"Didn't know what? What didn't you know?"

Ruth opened her mouth, then closed it. "Jamie, I...I..." She buried her face in her hands and vanished.

Jamie spun in a tight circle, "I'm sorry if I said something I shouldn't have, Ruth...Ruth...ah hell." She felt bad for bringing up a topic that was apparently very upsetting. "Way to go, dummy," she whispered to herself as she kicked the dirt. Nothing like scaring off a ghost to kill one's self-esteem.

With her helmet tucked securely under her arm, Kali pushed the glass door open and walked into the southwest division office of Legacy Lesbians. It was a relatively small office that shared space with twelve other businesses in an older strip mall off the town's busy main road. The interior was bright blue, with framed posters of the many events Legacy Lesbians hosted. Celebrities and ridiculously gorgeous women smiled at the camera as they cruised, hiked, rafted, rode horses, went whale watching, and attended concerts, golf events, and much more. Legacy events were well-known in the women's community and had a reputation for almost always selling out. Which surprised Kali, considering their events were a bit pricey. The sole reason why she had yet to go to one. Who had that kind of extra money? She sure didn't. But apparently, lesbians seemed glad to pay a premium to know they would be surrounded by their own.

"Well, well, well, look what the wind blew in," Paige announced as she leaned against the door frame of her modestly sized office.

"Hey, Paige."

Paige motioned with a tilt of her head for Kali to step inside. Damn, she's sexy, Kali thought as she licked her lips while she checked out the black dress tightly wrapped around Paige's curvy body.

They'd met in the restroom line of the local women's bar one night. Twenty minutes later, as they'd emerged, they were fully engaged in conversation. By the end of the evening, they'd been joined at the hip on the dance floor and joined everywhere else later in Kali's bedroom. By the time they'd returned to the land of the living, late the next day, Paige had told Kali she was head over heels for her.

But as hot as the sex was, Kali hadn't wanted to get involved in another relationship. She was still in protection mode, and that meant a chastity belt was locked around her heart. Placed there five years ago when her ex had left to be with someone who could afford to give her the lifestyle Kali could not. Jaded, deflated, untrusting, and not wanting anything more than a distraction, Kali had only wanted sex. She had turned into a lesbian cliché, and she knew it. Sadly, it had taken Paige a month before she'd finally given up the chase and another six months before agreeing to be friends.

"Have a seat." Paige motioned to the two chairs facing her desk. Kali placed her helmet on one, took her backpack off, then scooted the other closer to the desk.

"You look great Paige."

"Marriage suites me. Who knew? Although, it hasn't been the best for my waistline."

"Trust me, you look sexy as ever. Your wife is very lucky." A twinge of jealousy hit her. Paige was beautiful, hot as hell in the bedroom, and had her shit together. *Why did I throw that away?*

Paige chuckled. "Still the charmer, I see."

"I mean it, Paige. She's lucky to have you."

"And I, her. Now, let's talk about this vineyard."

"It'll make the perfect setting for weddings and receptions." Kali pulled her cell phone out, leaned over the desk, and presented Paige with a slideshow.

"Looks quaint," Paige said.

"It is." Kali beamed with pride. It was the first time in her life she was a part of something that felt so rewarding. Something that she thought mattered in life.

"So." Paige leaned back in her chair, signaling that she was satisfied with the look of the place. "You said in your message that you live on this property? Catch me up."

Kali nodded. "I do. Jamie was one of two people who inherited the land from her aunt when she died. It's a fifty-acre vineyard, with a vintage Victorian house that overlooks prime views of the Sonoma County hills. And the main attraction is that it's owned and operated by lesbians." Kali cocked her arms to her chest to reference herself. "Jamie knew how miserable I was at the TV station, so she asked me if I wanted to work the vineyard with her. I think I said yes before she finished the sentence."

Kali had become burned out on a business that cherry-picked the most sensationalized stories and turned them into the news of the day. It was an environment that focused on the brutal and the bizarre, and Kali had been tired of hearing about the dark side of mankind. It had started to make her even more jaded.

"Nice friend."

"Yeah, she's the best." Kali glanced at the framed photos on Paige's desk. Frozen moments in time of Paige and her wife stared back. A shiver made its way up Kali's spine as she thought about the night they had been together. Paige was an amazing kisser, the best Kali had been with so far. *It may have been just one night, but that night made one hell of an impression.* But deep down, she knew Paige was in a better place. Still.

"Tell you what, I'll email you a contract. Look it over, and if the terms suit you, you can digitally sign it and get it back to me. Once that happens, I'll put you in touch with Victoria, our coordinator. She will be the go-between for you and the client."

Kali jumped off her chair, beaming with excitement. "Does that mean you'll include us on your website?"

Paige chuckled as she stood and walked around her desk. "Yes, that means we'll promote your vineyard as one of our recommended venues for weddings and receptions."

"I could kiss you right now."

Paige blushed as she extended her hand. "This is the safer alternative for both of us. Good to see you again, Kali. I'll send the contract by end of day."

Kali pushed her hand away and gave her a warm hug. "Thanks," she whispered in a genuine tone as her body responded to Paige pressing against her.

"You're welcome," Paige finally said as she cleared her throat and broke the embrace. "Come on. I'll walk you to the door."

Kali picked up her backpack and shoved her helmet under her arm.

"Don't be a stranger. Michelle and I would love to have you over for dinner one night." Paige pushed the door open and held it as a woman dashed inside, bumping right into Kali.

"Oops, I'm so sorry, I didn't see you," the woman said.

"No worr—" Kali stopped midsentence and stared. The woman had flawless dark skin, a thin chiseled face with a slight cleft chin, piercing green eyes, and dark short hair that parted perfectly down the middle.

Kali did a doubletake as she stood in stunned silence. There, standing before her was the woman she conjured up every time she used her vibrator. The woman who satisfied every inch of her fantasies. The woman Kali thought couldn't possibly exist outside her mind.

"Kali, this is Victoria. Victoria, Kali," Paige said.

Kali reached out without taking her eyes off Victoria's face. "Nice to meet you," she said as they shook hands.

"Uh-huh." Victoria continued to stare.

Paige leaned in and cleared her throat in Kali's ear.

"Oh, um, yep. I, uh, I guess I better get going. It was nice to meet you, Victoria." Kali backed out the door Paige was still patiently holding and three steps later, tripped down the curb to her motorcycle.

"Uh-huh," Victoria repeated as Paige waved Kali off and closed the door.

❖

Kate paused beside the small blue lamp shattered in three pieces by the end table in the main room. "Thought you said it was safe?"

"It is," Jamie mumbled as she sat deep in the couch, taking her focus off the laptop balanced on her thighs. "Buddy knocked that over while going after a fly buzzing around the lampshade. I'll clean it up in a minute. As for Kali"— she nodded to the ceiling—"it took a while for her to calm down, but she's been test driving her new toy for the past half hour."

"Well, that's a good sign."

"I thought so too."

Kate walked over to the coffee table and turned the TV on. "Well, that's another good sign." She motioned toward a perfect screen, void of the slightest glitch or flicker.

"Huh." Jamie sighed as she placed her laptop on the table.

"What's up?" Kate picked up the broken pieces of the lamp and walked them into the kitchen.

"Well, I started out researching everything I could about ghost sightings and paranormal behavior, but now, I'm trying to find some type of documentation on any murder that might have taken place on this land. But there doesn't seem to be any record of anything. If Ruth was murdered here, no one bothered to record anything about it." Since their last encounter, she'd become obsessed with Ruth. The more she thought about her, the more her body responded. And the more her body responded, the more she felt like her grip on reality was slipping. *I have feelings for a dead person who was rumored to be a horse thief.* Not the best opening line to admit to anyone when filling them in on your latest crush.

"You saw Ruth again?" Kate returned with a bottle of Pinot Noir, two glasses, and a corkscrew sticking halfway out of her front pocket. She plopped on the couch and placed the glasses on the coffee table.

"Yeah, this morning, right after you and Ginger took off. I asked her what happened that night."

"And?" Kate placed the bottle between her thighs as she twisted the corkscrew in.

"And nothing. She got really upset and then she just… disappeared." The familiar pop sound brought a smile to

Jamie's face, and Kate poured the wine into the one glass and slid it over.

"Maybe she doesn't want to talk about it."

"Obviously. I just hope I didn't scare her off for good. I didn't mean to be insensitive." The look on Ruth's face when Jamie had asked about her past was haunting. She knew that look. It was the look she had every time her mind yanked her down some painful memory lane. If Ruth was anything like Jamie, reliving a memory could sometimes be worse than the actual event. Although in Ruth's case, considering the outcome, maybe not.

"I've never known you to be insensitive, so I'm sure it wasn't that."

"Wasn't what?" Kali bounded down the stairs.

"Grab a glass and join us," Kate said as she leaned back into the cushion.

"Kate was just saying I could never be insensitive," Jamie said as Kali emerged from the kitchen, wineglass in hand.

Kali snorted as she sat. "I think stealing a very personal item from someone qualifies as being insensitive."

"Your vibrator was becoming a nuisance."

"Hey, that vibrator was the only thing getting me through singlehood." Kali poured, leaned back, and put her bare feet on the table.

Jamie scoffed. "Ever think of taking up a hobby?"

"Already got one."

"Masturbation isn't a hobby." Jamie giggled as she took another sip and entertained a fond memory of the many enjoyable toys that inhabited the storage container she and Cheryl had hidden under their bed. Yet another thing lost in the breakup. "We good?" She nudged Kali with her shoulder.

Kali clinked their glasses. "Yeah, we're good."

Jamie leaned in and kissed her on the cheek. "I love you."

"Love you too." Kali smiled. "So I have a proposal. After I left Legacy, I went over to Chanadoah Winery and asked Mick what he would charge to bottle wine for our private label."

"*Our* private label?" Jamie asked.

"Mm-hmm." Kali held up her hand. "Just hear me out. Now that we'll have Legacy promoting us, I got thinking we really should have our own private label to serve and sell. And we can give the happy couple a bottle to take with them. A remembrance of their ceremony at the vineyard."

Jamie nodded. What a brilliant idea. Any souvenir was added advertising for the vineyard. If the happy couple displayed the bottle for friends to see, the ripple effect could mean more bookings.

"At first, I was thinking we could call our wine Les Wine About It or Women Squared, you know, as in woman to woman. But then I thought we should just call it Three Friends, in honor of us."

"How about Four Friends?" Kate suggested in a faraway voice. "That way, we can honor Nora as well."

❖

Years ago, Kate had the same idea about creating a private label. On the day she had been going to talk to Nora about expanding the reach of the vineyard, Nora had come home with news of her cancer.

"How long?" Kate had asked as they'd sat on the couch, holding hands and crying.

"They said if I make it two more years, I'll be lucky," Nora had choked out as she'd squeezed Kate's hand in fear.

Kate had leaned over and embraced her, hoping to absorb her fear. But her own had coursed through her veins too as she'd thought of the possibility of losing the part of her life that made her feel complete. And of all things, damn it, why did it have to be cancer that had come knocking?

Damn it, Kate had cried through silent tears, this had not been the way Nora had wanted to go out. She had always hoped she would die dancing, not from a disease that horrifically striped the essence of her soul out from under her.

❖

Jamie nodded to Kate. "I think that would be very nice."

"Four Friends, it is. I'll work on some design options for the label, and we can vote on which one we like the best."

"I'm sure they'll all be wonderful." Jamie patted Kali on the thigh, grabbed her glass, and headed for the door. For a brief moment, she thought about staying and going over design ideas with Kali, something they always did back in their newsroom days when Jamie produced the nightly show, and Kali handled the graphics. But Jamie had been thinking of Ruth nonstop since their talk early that morning, and since her Google searches hadn't provided much information, she was anxious and hopeful that she might see Ruth again tonight so they could talk some more. And if she was perfectly honest with herself, the more she thought about Ruth, the more her mind transformed her into a living person. Someone that she could explore in a flesh on flesh kind of way. Providing the rest of Ruth looked as real as the part Jamie had seen.

"I'll be out on the front porch if you need me. The night is too beautiful to stay in."

"I'll join—"

Kate coughed over Kali's words and muttered something.

Jamie turned. "What did you say?"

"Uh, nothing, go enjoy the evening."

Jamie nodded as she walked out to the porch. Her body reacted as she approached the bench. Hopefully, she hadn't scared Ruth off too much, and this evening would hold another magical encounter with the woman who was rapidly taking up a lot of real estate in Jamie's mind.

She plopped on the bench, took a sip of wine, and enjoyed the bright glow the moon cast over the land. Within minutes, the sound of approaching footsteps sent the butterflies in her stomach into flight.

"Thought I'd show up the right way this time." Ruth smiled as she approached. "That seat taken?" She nodded to the empty spot.

"It just so happens, I was kinda saving it for you." Jamie patted the space.

Ruth slowly walked up the steps. "Sorry about earlier. Sometimes when I get scared, I just kind of—"

"Vanish?"

Ruth flopped down, lowered her head, and nodded.

Jamie squinted as she examined Ruth's face. If she extended her finger to Ruth's cheek, would her finger pass through her, or would there be substance? *This is why you're driving me nuts.* Jamie scanned Ruth's body. *My mind knows you're a ghost, yet my eyes see you as real. And it's what I'm seeing that makes me want you.* "I hope I wasn't inappropriate in asking about—"

"No, no you weren't at all. It's just that, well, as you can imagine, thoughts of that night are still quite upsetting, even after all this time."

"That's just it, Ruth, I don't know anything about that night. Apparently, my great grandfather never told anyone what really happened."

"You mean, you really don't know?"

Jamie shook her head.

"So you don't know what those men did to me...what Hank was a part of?"

Again, Jamie shook her head and felt the need to apologize to Ruth. But apologize for what? What had her great-grandfather done?

"They murdered me." Ruth's eyes welled with tears. "They buried me over there." She pointed to the southeast corner of the land. "And afterward, they..." She choked on her words. "They..."

Jamie froze in stunned silence. Murdered? Did Ruth say she was murdered? *What the hell happened?* "What Ruth, what did they do?" Her heart hurt for Ruth as her head pounded with the information that her great grandfather was involved in a murder. *What could you have possibly done to deserve that?* "Ruth, I..." She leaned in to hold Ruth, but just before she made contact, Ruth began pulsing with light. "Jeezus, what the..." She jumped off the bench. Ruth turned between her normal skin tone to a pale light blue, then back again at the same pace as a rapid heartbeat.

"What?" Ruth sniffled, as she wiped her sleeve across her face.

"You're, um, you're pulsing blue."

Ruth glanced at her hands, then up to Jamie, who was backing away. "Please don't be frightened."

"Okay." Jamie felt stiff, as though cold water had just been thrown on her emotions.

"Jamie, please." Ruth pleaded as she stood and took a step. "I'm not a monster. You know I'm not."

Jamie held out her hand as she leaned against the banister, signaling Ruth not to come close. "I know you're not a monster Ruth, but right now, just give me a moment." The shiver surging through her body was causing her skin to crawl. It was easy to overlook the fact that Ruth was a ghost when she looked so alive, but watching her pulse was a slap back to reality.

Ruth sighed as she sat back down. "When I become extremely emotional, I pulse. I don't know why it happens, and I can't control it. The last time it happened was at Nora's ceremony."

Jamie recalled the small, celebration-of-life gathering they'd held at the vineyard for Nora. It had been just her, Kali, and Kate. As per Nora's instructions, they'd built a fire in the pit, thrown her ashes in, and toasted her life.

"I remember seeing you during her celebration-of-life ceremony. You were standing off to the side by the vines," Jamie cocked her head in the direction of the firepit as she tried to focus on a vision lodged deep in her memory. A blue pulse had come from Ruth, but at the time, Jamie had thought it was an illusion from the flicker of the flames. *Huh.* "And if I remember right, you were still there after the fire died down and we headed inside." Jamie remembered shuffling back to the house and the feeling of numbness from too much wine and crying. As she'd turned to look at the pit one last time, she'd thought she saw Ruth through blurry, tear stained eyes, stepping out from behind the vines and sitting on one of the four railroad ties that bordered the firepit.

"I stayed there all night. It was the least I could do. Nora was always so kind to me. She would make it a point every morning to wave to me while she was standing out here, doing some rather odd stretches."

Jamie chuckled, "Yoga."

"Excuse me?"

"Aunt Nora liked to do her morning yoga on the porch. It's, um, a form of exercise."

"Yoga," Ruth repeated. "Well, it didn't seem like a very active form of exercise."

"I think that's the point." Jamie noticed the pulsing had stopped. "Ruth?"

"Hmm?"

"Is Nora on this land, you know, as a ghost or something like that?" She held her breath in hope of a different answer than the one she already knew in her heart. *Please say yes.*

Ruth shook her head. "No. No one else is here. I'm all alone. Always have been."

"Oh." Jamie glanced at the floor in disappointment. She really hadn't thought Nora was here, but since Nora's memories were everywhere, Jamie hoped a part of her soul was too. "I didn't think so, but I thought I'd ask. Kate would want to know."

"I wish she was. I miss her. Even though I never interacted with her or Kate, I really enjoyed watching them." Ruth nodded in the direction of the firepit. "Did you know Nora would make a fire every week, then take her clothes off and dance naked under the stars. Kate would join her from time to time. They both seemed so…free. So…*alive.*"

"Naked? Kate and Aunt Nora? Under the stars?" The memories of Nora blasting the music in the house, drinking her wine and dancing, warmed her heart. Maybe Aunt Nora was right; maybe life wasn't worth living if you couldn't dance your way through it. "She used to always tell me dancing was life's true form of expression."

Ruth shyly smiled. "Well, she expressed herself pretty openly at the firepit. I didn't mean to invade their privacy by watching, but they seemed to be having so much fun giggling and dancing with their arms in the air." Ruth lifted her arms, waved them around, and bounced on the bench. "They looked so ridiculous at times that I just couldn't turn away."

Jamie let out a belly laugh. *Good God, Ruth is adorable.* "That's what we call a train wreck, and Aunt Nora had a lot of them." She pushed off the banister and shuffled back to the bench. "I'm sorry for my reaction just now. I didn't—"

"It's okay, I understand," Ruth said dejectedly. "I mean, look at me, I don't even know who I am anymore or what I am. I watched those men bury my body. I shouldn't even be here. And yet, here I am, and I have no clue why." She poked at her body, "I can feel, walk, run, laugh and cry, obviously." She snorted. "I look alive, yet I have no heartbeat. I can hold things, kick things, and move things, yet I can't walk off this land. So much of me still feels so alive, yet I know I'm not. I wish I knew what it all meant, and why I'm really here, but I don't."

"Maybe you're still here because you have unfinished business." Jamie thought about herself. If she died today, she'd have a laundry list of unfinished business. Hell, her whole life felt unfinished. *Great, based on that theory, I'll never make it to my final destination.*

Ruth shook her head. "I really don't think so. If there is unfinished business out there that I need to tend to, why can't I leave this land? I think there's another explanation, I just don't know what it is. Meanwhile, I'm just…" She frowned as she hunched her shoulders. "Stuck."

"So you never made it to…you know." Jamie pointed up.

"Nope, I've never made it off this land. I keep waiting, though, and hoping that someday, I will be able to leave, but so far…nothing."

Jamie couldn't begin to comprehend what Ruth was going through. Yet in her own way, she could definitely relate to feeling like she was just putting in time, going through the motions. She picked up her wineglass and took a sip as information from the websites about ghosts danced in her head. She'd read dozens of articles with scientific explanations, theories, and myths about ghosts. Most said sightings were a result of overactive imaginations or tricks. Other articles pointed to some sort of religious component to reason them away. But any real evidence of their presence was pretty much nonexistent.

And yet, here Ruth sat. Jamie took another sip. Maybe Ruth had fallen through the cracks, and someone had forgotten to collect her soul? A clerical error of sorts. Jamie chuckled at the thought and noticed Ruth staring at her glass. "Oh, I would offer you a drink but…"

Ruth grabbed the glass and emptied it in three quick gulps. She wiped her sleeve across her mouth, then let out a loud burp. "Wow, that tasted good."

"I…um…I, huh, you can drink?"

"And eat…or not. Obviously, I don't need to for survival, but I can still taste things. And no matter how much I eat or drink, it never seems to affect me." She referenced her ghostly body. "It just kind of goes in, disappears, and never adds to or takes away from how I look."

"You know, I'm totally jealous of you right now." Ah, to have the pleasure of decadent taste without the consequences. *A pleasure that seems more appealing than sex.* Jamie chuckled as she focused on Ruth's tongue licking the last drop of red liquid from her lips. *Or not.* How was it that she could be so turned on right now? And not just a little bit, but full-on shiver up the spine and erect nipples, turned on. Jamie nibbled on her lip as the thought of kissing Ruth played out in her head. Would her lips be as soft as they looked? Would they feel cold as ice or warm and inviting? Would they...but before she let another overanalyzed thought cross her mind, she leaned in to Ruth's beautiful, kissable lips, and Ruth began to pulse.

But just as their lips were about to touch, the front screen door flew open, smashing against the side of the house, making a loud banging noise. Kate and Kali spilled onto the porch in one tangled human ball.

"What the..." Startled, Jamie jumped up, adrenaline rushing through her blood. "What's wrong?"

"Sorry," Kali said as she rolled off Kate. "Sorry about that. Nothing's wrong. Everything's cool."

Jamie turned to see if Ruth was as rattled as she was, but the bench was empty. Her shoulders slumped as she sat. "Shit," she whispered under a frustrated breath. "Well, if nothing's wrong, then what's going on?"

Kate said in a soft embarrassed voice, "Nothing."

"Yeah, nothing, why?" Kali repeated.

"You came crashing out the door, tumbling over one another like the house was on fire, and nothing's going on?"

"Yep, all good." Kali smiled. "How are *you* doing?"

Jamie's edge faded as she chuckled. "Oh, I see. You were spying on us from the door, weren't you?" She couldn't really blame them. She probably would have done the same.

"I'm insulted." Kali shuffled over and flopped on the bench.

"Uh-huh." Jamie smiled as she nudged her shoulder.

"Oh, hell, Jamie," Kate said. "I filled Kali in on Ruth, and when we heard you talking out here, we figured she'd showed up, so we just kind of—"

"We wanted to check you two out," Kali interrupted. "We were craning our necks trying to get a peek when Kate lost her balance and took me down with her."

"*You're* the one who lost their balance, not me."

Kali placed her hand on her chest, "Why, Kate Spalding, I'm offended."

"Yeah, like that's possible." Kate rolled her eyes. "So where'd she go?"

"I think the commotion scared her off."

"We're sorry, Jamie," Kali said in an apologetic tone.

"It's okay." Jamie put an arm around her. "I have a feeling she didn't go far." She glanced into the night. Something told her Ruth was close by, probably standing in the shadows, just out of sight. She was still aroused, and a part of her wanted to break away from her friends, find Ruth, and finish what had been interrupted. But as Jamie glanced at Kali and Kate, she settled deeper into the bench and leaned into Kali. She almost kissed a ghost tonight. The thought was equal parts exciting and frightening. "So…Kate?" She glanced over at the firepit.

"Hmm?"

"Dancing under the stars, firepit…naked." Jamie put her arms up in the air and moved them around. "Ring a bell?"

Kate's eye's widened.

"Kate? Care to fill us in?" Jamie teased.

"No fair telling secrets," Kate shouted to the vineyard, then turned to Jamie and Kali. "I'm suddenly feeling tired." She faked a yawn. "Think I'll go to bed, see you two in the morning."

"Kate, you turn right back around and spill," Jamie demanded.

Kate hurried to the door and dashed inside.

"The truth shall set you free," Jamie yelled after her and wondered what it would be like to live a life so free and uninhibited.

"I'm already free, and truth had nothing to do with it." Kate's words traveled out onto the porch. "Night."

When Jamie turned, Kali was staring. "Nora and Kate dancing naked around the firepit?"

"Apparently."

"Wow…I imagine that must have been quite the sight."

"I think I'll pass on imagining it." Jamie thought of the two women she loved more than her own parents, dancing without a care in the world under the stars on a beautiful full moon night. She wondered if those were the moments Kate held in her mind when Jamie caught her with a faraway stare and a tear in her eye.

"So do you like her?" Kali asked.

"Who?"

"Ruth?"

"I...um, it's kinda complicated, Kali. Besides, there is that one little detail about her being a ghost and all."

"Yeah, I know, but do you *like* her?"

Jamie paused for a moment and finally said with a big smile, "Yeah, I do."

Kali returned a warm knowing smile and nodded. "So ghost sex, huh?"

"Kali!"

Kali laughed. "Well, not to turn the conversation around to me, but I'm going to. I think I may have found someone."

Jamie leaned back as she smiled. "What? When? Who?"

"Remember that night I drank way too much wine and told you about the woman I fantasized about every time I used my vibrator?"

"I do."

"Well, I found her. Her name's Victoria, and she's the event coordinator at Legacy. When I was there talking to Paige this morning, she walked in, and when I looked at her, it was like time just stopped. And check this, she has dark skin, a cleft chin, green eyes, and short dark hair that parts perfectly down the middle."

"Holy shit."

"I know, right?"

"Kali, I'm so happy for you."

"Thanks, but I mean, you know, I just met her and all, but there was just…"

"Something about her." Jamie finished Kali's sentence as she thought about Ruth.

"Yeah, and I can't—"

"Stop thinking about her?" Jamie whispered. *Maybe there's hope for us yet.*

"Mm-hmm."

Warmth filled Jamie's heart as thoughts of touching Ruth flew back into her head and began pecking away at her "never again" promise. She caught a glimpse of blue light flickering amongst the vines, and it made her smile. What if there really was a thin veil between life and death, allowing many categories of each to overlap? What if people had it all wrong about ghosts, the paranormal, and the afterlife? Death, she chuckled to herself, seemed to hold as many mysteries as life. And maybe that was what made both so intriguing.

❖

As Ruth looked on from behind the fullness of the grape leaves, she pulsed with a mixture of sadness and joy. She thought about the relationships she had been robbed of in life but was excited for the one that was beginning. She hoped things would develop further between her and Jamie, but she knew from past experience to never hang her hopes on love. She'd tried that twice, and the last one had gotten her murdered. But as Ruth watched Jamie and Kali sit on the bench together, engulfed in conversation, she became lost in Jamie's infectious smile, and it became clear to her what she had known for a while, what she had been fighting. Death had taken many things from her, but it hadn't taken her ability to feel emotions. And in that moment, she realized what she had known for the past several years. She had fallen in love with the adult version of that little girl who'd once run around the vineyard and given her so much joy.

Ruth slowly turned away and strolled down the row of vines. Maybe for the first time in a very long time, things were looking up.

Chapter Four

Kali and Jamie sat on opposite ends of the couch, silently staring at their phones. "Do you need any help, Kate?" Jamie called to the kitchen but didn't take her eyes off her screen. She had been surfing more websites with testimonies from people who claimed anything from living in a haunted house to communicating with the dead. The stories ranged from scary to comical, but none of the encounters came anywhere close to Ruth.

"Holy shit, someone's interested in getting married here." Kali flipped her phone around and extended her arm to show the screen.

Jamie looked up and squinted, "I can't read that."

Kate came out from the kitchen balancing three plates, each stacked with blueberry granola pancakes. "What did you just say?" She set the plates on the coffee table, then flopped on the couch.

"Paige just sent me a text. Two women want to get married here next month. It's a small group. Just the happy couple and about thirty friends and family."

"Next month? Kali, we're not ready to host a wedding that soon." Jamie tossed her phone on the table and motioned to Kate to pass the syrup. Gathering around the coffee table every morning and eating pancakes had become their morning ritual. What had started out as a temporary way to honor Nora's love for the breakfast food had settled into a daily habit they all looked forward to.

"And reception," Kali continued to read.

"What?" Jamie said with alarm.

Kate mumbled as she tried to talk around a bite. "I can make some calls to a few companies I've worked with before. They can string white lights, provide tables, linen and—"

"And I'll call Annie and get a quote on catering," Kali threw out.

"Annie?" Jamie asked as she picked up the soymilk and poured some in her coffee.

"I may or may not have spent an incredibly hot weekend with her a couple of years ago."

Jamie laughed. "Is there anyone you haven't slept with besides me and Kate?"

"The point is, she's a sous chef at Marlow's, she's a fantastic cook, she does catering on the side, and we're on good terms with each other."

"I don't know. Kali, we're not—"

"Don't, Jamie, just don't. You always have a way of panicking yourself out of something good. We signed the contract last night, agreeing the extra revenue would be a lifesaver for this place, so now's not the time to second-guess it. Besides, it's fucking Legacy Lesbians. It doesn't get much better than that."

Jamie took a moment to think. Did she really panic herself out of good things? It was true that she did freak out on every date her friends had tried to set her up with after Cheryl. And she had seriously panicked last night when Ruth had pulsed, but that was obviously different. And she did have that anxiety attack when she had been approached with an offer for a better position at a competing TV station. *Maybe Kali's right. Maybe I do panic myself out of something good.*

"I'm with Kali," Kate said as she shoved another forkful in her mouth.

"Okay…okay," Jamie conceded. Maybe it was finally time to start letting go of her crippling insecurities and the voices in her head that kept telling her she was never good enough, smart enough, or had her shit together enough. "Let's do it."

Kali whooped as she grabbed her phone. "Oh no." She scrunched her face.

"What's wrong? What is it?"

"Paige is sending Victoria to walk around the vineyard to get a feel for what we need." Kali lifted her arms and took a quick sniff under each armpit. "I need to shower." She hopped over the back of the couch and flew up the steps.

Kate forked Kali's untouched pancakes to her plate. "Victoria?"

"Kali's latest crush."

"Kinda figured when she threw out the whole, gotta take a shower, thing."

"Do you really think we'll be ready for this? I don't want a bad review our first time at bat."

"Don't worry, it's a small group. We have over a month to figure it all out. It'll be fine."

Jamie nodded. *Good ol' Kate.* She could always see a solution in every problem life threw at her. Jamie changed the topic. She wanted, no, needed to talk about the source of the insomnia that had tortured her all night. "Kate?"

"Mm-hmm?"

"I've known you as long as I can remember."

"You trying to make me feel old, or is this going somewhere?"

"If you ever thought I was, you know, kinda losing it around the edges, you'd tell me, right?"

Kate leaned back. "This have anything to do with our little ghost friend?" She pointed to Jamie with her fork.

"Maybe," she answered in an octave higher than her normal tone.

Kate took a sip of her coffee. "I'm all ears. What's got you spooked?"

"Wow, that was so not funny." *Great, now I'm going to become the butt of everyone's jokes.*

"Sure, it was, but please, continue."

"I, um, can't stop thinking about her. And last night on the porch, I almost kissed her."

"And that's a bad thing?"

A shotgun of confusing emotions exploded in Jamie's head. *Ruth looks real, yet she pulses blue. She doesn't have a heartbeat, yet she says she can feel sadness and joy. She's obviously dead, yet I can talk to her.* Several websites warned that ghosts could be temperamental and capable of horrible things, yet Ruth seemed a gentle, kind soul. The contradictions were giving her a headache. "Yes, it's a bad thing. She's a ghost!"

"Thought we already covered that."

"Yeah, but right now, there's something really specific I need to talk about." She raised her eyebrows and cocked her head.

"Oh God, you're doing the eyebrow thing again. Honey, I haven't had enough coffee yet to guess what it means this time, so why don't you just come out and say it?"

"Ghost sex," Jamie whispered.

Kate spat a piece of pancake out as she choked on laughter. She grabbed her coffee off the table, took a gulp, and pounded a bit on her chest. "Damn, girl, your mind does wander down some strange alleys."

"What? You haven't wondered about where things could be heading with me and Ruth?"

"I confess, my mind has gone there a time or two."

"Right...right."

Kate took another sip. "When I was in college, I fell madly in love with a woman I couldn't have. She was beautiful, spontaneous, and funny as hell. But she wasn't attracted to me 'in that way.'" She bent her fingers in air quotes. "So we were never physically together, but that didn't mean my love for her was any less. Love is love. Sometimes, you're given the gift of having the emotional as well as the physical. Sometimes, you just get the emotional. Hell, your last girlfriend was alive and—"

"I have many other words to describe her state of being." Jamie thought there wasn't a ghost out there that could one-up Cheryl. She didn't need to rattle chains or moan to make someone feel a bit crazy.

Kate chuckled, "I'm sure you do, but the point is… where'd that get you? Whatever you've got going on with Ruth, enjoy it. If it's possible for things to get physical, then go for it. If not, then enjoy the emotional. She's making your heart sing, Jamie. Follow the music. Life's too short. Besides, who's to say what's right or wrong when it comes to love? Hell, governments and religions have been telling us since the dawn of time who to love, and you know what I think about that."

"Fuck that shit," they said at the same time.

They both laughed as Kate stood and stretched.

"I'm going to go exercise Ginger." She grabbed her plate and cup. As she turned toward the kitchen, she placed a loving hand on Jamie's shoulder. "I'll tell you one thing, though."

"What's that?"

"It's nice to see you happy again."

"Even if I feel half-crazy?"

"Life would be pretty goddamn boring if we all colored within the lines."

Kate was right. The best parts of Jamie's life had always been when she'd wandered off the beaten path and discovered her own hidden treasures. Maybe it was time she started doing that again.

❖

Kate grabbed her old straw cowboy hat off the rack by the front door and headed over to the barn. Late last night, Jamie had filled her in on what Ruth had said about Nora's spirit not being on the land. The finality of Ruth's words had been a punch to Kate's gut. She'd been hoping beyond hope that a part of Nora was still here, linking the two of them somehow. But then again, maybe that meant Nora had transitioned over and was happily dancing somewhere up above. Still, she would have given anything to have her back on the land like Ruth. And have the opportunity to talk to and touch her again.

"Whatcha doing?" Kate pulled a chair next to Nora, who was sitting at the dining table, typing away on her laptop.

"Creating my will. Seems like you can do anything online these days. I'm giving you half the vineyard and Jamie half. But don't you dare sell this place to my brother or anyone else once I'm dead and gone, or I'll come back and haunt you forever. Both of ya's. You'd never get rid of me."

Kate reached around Nora's waist and hugged her tight. "Well, if it would bring you back to me, I just might be tempted." She nibbled the words softly in Nora's ear.

"Hush your mouth, Kate Spalding. Besides, you wouldn't want to deal with the side of me that would have to come storming back here from my grave."

Kate chuckled. "You know I would never sell this land and neither would your niece."

"I know, and that's why I love you." She leaned back and kissed her.

"That the only reason?"

"That and the way your ass moves in those tight jeans." She kissed Kate again.

"Keep this up, and I'm going to have table sex with you."

Nora slowly got up, scooted her laptop aside, sat on the table, and spread her legs. "Baby, you know how much I love table sex."

"I do."

"If I ever come back to haunt you, you better make sure there's a table around."

"I will," Kate leaned in, unbuttoned Nora's jeans, glided a hand in her underwear, and entered her as she kissed Nora hard.

Kate pulled the barn door open as Ginger whinnied. "I'm coming, I'm coming." She walked over to the mini fridge in the corner and pulled out a handful of carrots. As she handed one to Ginger, she decided she didn't completely accept what Ruth had said about Nora. There were too many times she'd felt her presence. Somehow, someway, Nora was still here. Maybe that was wishful thinking, but it was what made Kate's heart feel at peace. And right now, that was exactly what she needed.

❖

"I was a runaway." Ruth slowly walked up to Jamie, who was holding a grape up to the sun.

Jamie turned to face her. "I'm sorry?"

Ruth stopped within ten feet. "I said I was a runaway." She sat and crossed her legs. She took a deep uncomfortable breath, shoved her right hand into the top layer of soil, and let it slowly rain through her fingers.

"My father was a preacher in Oregon and my mom a school teacher. According to my dad, they were very much in love. My mom got pregnant right away. The first of many, they hoped." She paused and looked at Jamie. "But there was a complication with my birth. My mom bled out and died shortly after I was born. They had been married less than a year, and her loss sent my father into a deep depression. I think he blamed me for her death because he all but abandoned me. A few of the women from church noticed, and they ended up taking turns tending to me around the clock. I owed them my life.

"When I turned six, my father remarried a local seamstress named Mildred. She was quite a bit older than my father, and she tended to him like a doting mother would her child. But her kindness and attentiveness stopped with him. I was not extended the same affection or courtesies. Mildred was an evil and wretched woman, which I said several times to my father. But he didn't listen to a word. Instead, he let Mildred raise me as she saw fit. So away from his knowing eyes, she would whip me with a stick if I cleaned the house wrong, wore clothes unbefitting a preacher's daughter, spoke out of turn, or overslept. Once, she put the stick to me after I followed a squirrel up a tree because I wanted to see where it lived."

Ruth paused, still debating how much she should say. How much of herself she should expose. When she had been alive, no one had cared enough about her to ask, and that had been fine by her. The less people who knew about her, the better. But with Jamie, she wanted to talk. She wanted to tell this woman who was now sitting knee to knee with her in the dirt who she once was. What kind of life she'd once lived.

"Anyway, when I turned fifteen, I started having feelings for a woman whose family had recently moved into a house down the road. Her name was Jean, she was sixteen, and she was amazing. I spent as much time as possible with her. I guess you could say we became best friends, but deep down, I knew we were becoming so much more. And so did Mildred. She decided to put a stop to it one night before her and my father went out to an event. She came into my room when I was in the middle of changing clothes and beat *the bad* out of me. She whipped me over and over until I fell unconscious.

"When I came to, the house was dark and quiet. I knew that night that I had to get away. So I cleaned myself up, cut my hair off, stole some of my father's clothes, took as much food as I could stuff in a sack, and ran away. I changed my name to Thomas because I figured if I was going to make it on my own, I'd have a better shot if I looked like a boy. I was right. I was able to pick up odd jobs here and there until I made my way to California, where I signed on as a stable hand at a horse ranch. The owners were kind enough to let me sleep in their barn while I tended their horses. I had food, shelter, and a job I loved. I was the happiest I had ever been."

Jamie leaned back on her arms. "Did they know you were a girl?"

"If they did, nothing was said. I did my job, and I did it well. The horses loved me, and I loved them. I kept my head down and stayed out of everyone's way, and for ten years, the arrangement worked out just fine. But then Mr. Jenkins, the owner, died in a hunting accident. The property was sold, and I was not asked to stay on, so I headed down this way. It took a while, but eventually, I got a job at Parson's, a little general store just down the road." She pointed in the direction of a place no doubt long-ago demolished.

"I swept the floors, helped people out with their supplies, made sure the rodents didn't get in the grain sacks, and stuff like that. I kept my hair short, wore men's clothes, had a hat to hide my face, and kept my head down so no one could get a good look at me. I also rarely spoke. Most people thought I was simple in the head, so they didn't pay me much mind, which was fine by me. Things were going well for me until early one summer morning, Lillian Ross walked into the store." She trailed off as she became lost in memory.

"Thomas, go sweep the floor where the coffee beans spilled," Mr. Parson said from behind the counter as he tended to a customer. Ruth nodded, grabbed the broom, and began sweeping the loose beans into a pile on the pitted wooden

floor. As she bent to sweep the beans onto a piece of paper, a woman backed into her, making her lose her balance and tumble to the floor.

"Oh, my heavens, I am so sorry, I must not have—" The beautiful woman spun and hovered over Ruth, who was struggling to retrieve her hat an arms-length away. "You must forgive my clumsiness."

"No worries, ma'am," Ruth mumbled in as deep a voice as she could without sounding ridiculous. She jumped to her feet, grabbed her hat, placed it on her head, and continued looking down as she concentrated on brushing off her trousers.

"My name is Lillian, Lillian Ross, and please, you must let me..." She stopped mid-sentence as a sack of beans hit the counter with a bang. They both looked toward the front of the store.

"I should probably go help," Ruth mumbled as she stepped away.

"Well, now, what do we have here?"

Ruth paused and glanced at Lillian. Their eyes locked in a stare for a brief moment until Ruth's fear caused her to look down.

Lillian held a lace-covered hand under Ruth's chin and gently raised her head. They stood for a moment, staring intently at the other, Lillian in her two-tone, blue, high society dress; beautiful feathered hat; and matching lace umbrella. She had long, curly black hair and light brown eyes. She was tall and sported the perfect hourglass figure. She was the most beautiful woman Ruth had ever seen.

"Everything okay back there, Thomas?" Mr. Parson called.

Ruth raised her hand high and waved that all was well. "I, um, I have to go." She dashed out the back door and leaned against a pile of grain sacks as she caught her breath. She didn't want to linger outside too long, Mr. Parson probably needed her help, but she couldn't go back in quite yet. After what seemed like a reasonable amount of time for Lillian to leave, Ruth peeked her head around the door frame and scanned the store. There was no sign of her.

For the rest of that day, fear and excitement comingled in the pit of Ruth's stomach every time she heard someone walk into Parson's. Would it be the beautiful woman who smelled of freshly picked spring flowers, and if so, would she expose who Ruth really was? Or would they share another moment like the one she couldn't get out of her head? Lillian had awoken emotions deep within her, emotions buried after Mildred's last beating. The scars she carried from that night were a harsh reminder of what the world thought of people like her.

Two weeks had gone by, and Ruth had all but lost hope of ever seeing Lillian again when a hand caressed her forearm as she was placing bolts of fabric on a shelf. She knew who it was before she turned. She smiled as her stomach tightened.

"Your secret is safe with me."

"I'm Ruth."

"I must say, you have everyone here fooled. But a woman can always spot another by her eyes, and Ruth...you have the most gorgeous eyes."

Ruth blushed. "Thank you."

"Thomas," Mr. Parson yelled from somewhere within the store, "help Mrs. Willow out with her groceries."

Ruth looked at Lillian, "I have to go."

"Do you know the large oak tree that sits at the edge of town? Just past the barber and through the wheat field?"

Ruth nodded. "The one by old man Hank's land?"

"Yes, I'll be there this evening. Join me if you'd like."

"I'll be there," Ruth whispered as she hurried toward the front of the store.

Ruth stood, reached in her back pocket, and pulled out a small black and white photo. She paused to glance at the picture as Jamie stood, wiped the dirt from her pants, and craned her neck as if to get a glimpse of the photo. "That's Lillian." Ruth handed the photo to her and tapped on the figure wearing a dark dress, with a petite hat fashionably tilted on her head. Standing next to her was Ruth wearing dark pants; a white, button-down, collared shirt; suspenders; a dark, tailored jacket; and a newsboy hat. They were looking at each other and smiling.

"It was taken the week before I died, in another town about a three hour walk from here.

By that time, Lillian and I had been meeting up with one another for about a month."

"Ruth, isn't this place magical?"

"Yes," Ruth answered. A touch of claustrophobia came over her as she dodged a constant flurry of people, bicyclists, and horse carriages.

"I come here from time to time to buy the candy and dry goods Mr. Parson doesn't carry at your store. Today, you're in for a treat. Follow me." Lillian hurried down the wood sidewalk to a store. The swinging sign above the entrance read Smith's Candies. And as they entered, Ruth was hit with the overwhelming sweet smells of sugar treats.

"Good afternoon," a stocky bald man said.

"Good afternoon," Lillian replied.

Ruth kept her head down and hidden under her hat as she nodded. She didn't like getting out of her comfort zone and mingling with the public. Especially a public that didn't know her as Thomas, the simple-minded young man who hardly talked and stayed to himself. The people in this town would want to talk to her and expect her to talk back. A thought that made her very uncomfortable.

"Here." The man presented a tray of cherry colored, gooey squares. "We're kind of known for our taffy." They both took one.

Ruth moaned as the sugar, butter, and fruit exploded in her mouth.

"We'll take a bag of those, please and another of your licorice, oh, and a bag of chocolate squares, please." Lillian pointed to the candies.

"Good choices, madam." The clerk handed over several small bags stuffed with treats.

Lillian gestured to Ruth. "Have some."

Ruth gently took a piece of chocolate from one of the bags and popped it in her mouth, careful to keep her head low as the clerk rang Lillian up.

"Excuse me." A young man stepped from behind drawn curtains, startling Ruth. "Would you like your picture taken?" He held out a small black box.

Ruth had heard customers at Mr. Parson's talk about personal cameras that were all the rage but had never seen one. Just as she shook her head, Lillian chimed in.

"Oh, let's do it."

"I don't know, Lillian, I think that's a mistake," Ruth whispered, still fearful of publicly expressing too much of their affection.

"Don't be silly." Lillian waved her off as she turned to the man. "How much?"

"Thirty cents, and I can do it right here. You'll be the last photo on my roll, so I'll get right to it."

"Thirty cents is—"

"Is just fine." Lillian handed the man a few coins. "My cousin Thomas and I would love our picture taken."

"Yes, ma'am, thank you, ma'am, right this way." The young man escorted them to the back of the store, "Now just stand against that wall there." Ruth and Lillian shuffled over and stood shoulder to shoulder.

The young man held the black box chest high and looked into the viewer on the top. "A little closer, if you wouldn't mind." He motioned for Lillian to squeeze in a bit.

"We wouldn't mind at all," Lillian said. Ruth felt her cheeks blush. The proximity was causing her hands to sweat and her stomach to flutter.

"Okay, now look this way."

Ruth pulled her shoulders back and slightly raised her head.

"Okay, one, two…"

Lillian wrapped her pinkie around Ruth's. The surprising touch made her turn toward Lillian, who smiled back as the man snapped the photo.

"I should have it ready in about an hour."

"We will be dining at the Evans Hotel for lunch. We'll come by afterward to pick it up."

"Yes ma'am, that will be just fine."

Ruth grabbed their bags of candy, hustled out behind Lillian, and crossed the street. As soon as they entered the opulent hotel, Ruth felt uncomfortable. White linens, impeccably dressed wait staff, and chandeliers? She glanced at her clothes and felt embarrassed.

"Please follow me," a man instructed as he escorted them to a quaint table off to the side by the wall. Ruth pulled Lillian's chair out first, then her own. The host paused until they were settled, then handed each a menu.

Ruth opened the menu, and her jaw dropped. "Lillian, I, um, I can't afford—"

"You hush now. This is my treat."

"But…"

"I don't want to hear another word about it, you hear me," Lillian said in a kindhearted way.

Ruth hated the fact that Lillian was paying for everything. It just wasn't right. Even though they were both women, she was playing the part of the man. She was the one who should be paying. But on the meager wages she was making at Mr. Parson's, she could barely afford her own room and board.

"Madam?" The waiter approached, holding a piece of paper and pencil in hand.

"I shall have the squab chicken en cocotte."

"Excellent choice, and for you, sir?"

Ruth felt an anxiety attack coming on as she stared at the menu. She had never been in a fancy restaurant before, so she had no clue what any of the main courses were. "I, um," she mumbled as sweat began to bead on her face. "Um…"

"My cousin Thomas will have the broiled beef with vegetables and horseradish sauce, and could we also have enough creamed carrots for both of us, oh and um, a souffle Rothschild and poached pears in vanilla for dessert." She winked at Ruth.

"Thank you," Ruth mouthed.

"Right away, madam." The waiter nodded as he took their menus and left them alone.

"Now then, Ruth, since I have shared so much of myself with you over these past few weeks, might I ask you for the same?"

"What do you mean?" Ruth had been dreading the day Lillian would ask about her past. She didn't want to lie, but the thought of telling the truth made her feel like vomiting.

"What I mean is, tell me your fondest memory."

Ruth squirmed. Her fondest memory? Did she even have one? "I, um, I really can't recall any right now."

Lillian chuckled. "None? How is that even possible? Surely there must be one?"

"Okay, um." Ruth quickly scanned her life. She ruled out her childhood and all of her adult life…until now. Ruth placed her elbows on the table as she leaned in. "My fondest memory is the day the most beautiful woman I have ever seen accidently bumped into me at Parson's."

Lillian's cheeks turned a brighter shade of pink. "You are cheating at this game."

"Not at all. It's the truth. You're the first good thing that's happened to me."

"You are a charmer, aren't you?"

The waiter came over and placed the food in front of them. Ruth grabbed her fork and knife and took a moment to stare at a plate that looked like a work of art. She took a bite, slowly chewed, then glanced at Lillian. "This is the second-best thing that's happened in my life. This is wonderful."

Ruth chewed as slowly as possible to savor the food and company. When they were done and the plates had been cleared, dessert arrived, and again, Ruth couldn't believe the combination of flavors that exploded in her mouth. She wished this moment would last forever. But as the time lingered, she could sense Lillian becoming restless. "Is there somewhere else we need to be?"

Lillian pulled a pocket watch from her handbag and checked it a second time. "I believe the day has gotten away from me. I really must head back."

Ruth nodded at the words she dreaded hearing. As they stood to leave, she took one last glance around. She wanted to memorize every inch of the place, so she could call upon it in her dreams.

As they walked into the street, Ruth turned to Lillian. "Should we check on our picture?"

"Do me a favor and collect it, would you? I really must be off."

"Would you like me to see you to the stables?"

"Not necessary. I will be fine." She paused as she gazed at Ruth, "I wish I could give you a ride, but—"

"I understand all too well, Lillian." If anyone saw them from their small town, tongues could start flapping. "I've been on foot my whole life. I can manage the walk home just fine." The dance they were playing was a dangerous one, and they needed to be careful. "Lillian, I…" She stared into Lillian's eyes as her heart raced. Everything inside her wanted to kiss this beautiful woman. To show her what she meant, to express to her that Ruth had never been happier than when she was around Lillian. "I, um, thank you for a day that I will never forget."

Lillian smiled as she gently ran a hand down Ruth's cheek. "I shall always cherish these memories." She hurried toward the stables.

Ruth remained frozen as she watched the person who was stealing her heart get lost in the sea of people. If only they were able to share a life, how wonderful that would be. But all they would probably ever have would be stolen moments in time. Lillian was a refined woman, and Ruth had nothing to offer but her love. She turned and rapidly walked to the store. She wanted to get back home before dark.

"How was your lunch at the Evans, sir?"

Ruth kept her head down and her eyes hidden as she nodded.

"Very good. Well." The clerk handed her a small black and white photo. "Here is your photo."

Ruth cupped it and slowly traced her finger over Lillian's face.

"I hope you're pleased with it."

Again, Ruth nodded as she tipped her hat to the clerk and walked into the street. Never before had her heart beaten so fast, and her stomach fluttered so much, as when their fingers touched. Lillian was finding a special place in Ruth's heart. Maybe the next time she saw her, Ruth would tell her about her developing feelings. Yes. She began to put more confidence in her stride. Maybe it was time to do something about the way she was feeling. *Maybe the next time she saw Lillian, she would act on her feelings.*

Ruth placed the photo back in her pocket.

"Were you two together?" Jamie asked.

"No," Ruth answered, looking far away. "But everything inside me wished it. And I think it was the same for Lillian. But we were never given the opportunity."

"Why not?"

Ruth let out a long sigh. "Late one afternoon, Lillian came into the store to buy some grain…"

Ruth felt the familiar hand slip something into her front pocket, and it caused her entire body to tingle. Careful to keep her focus, she didn't turn right away. When she did, Lillian was up front with Mr. Parson, asking about a pound of grain. With Mr. Parson distracted, Ruth ducked behind several sacks of dried beans. She pulled out Lillian's note and studied the handwriting, tracing every word as they instructed her to meet at the usual tree late in the afternoon. Her body filled with joy. Tonight was the night she would kiss Lillian, she just knew it.

She hurried through the last of her chores, changed into new boots, brown tweed pants with black suspenders, and a collared white shirt. She briskly walked to the outskirts of the town, only slowing to pick a handful of purple wildflowers. As soon as she passed the barbershop, she took a hard left and sprinted through patches of wheat until she reached the large oak tree. She took a moment to run her fingers through her hair and smooth down her clothes before stepping into the clearing. Her heart lurched when she saw Lillian sitting on a blanket, her dress spread perfectly around her. She was taking food out of a wicker basket, looked up, and caught Ruth's eyes. "My, don't you look sharp."

"Nothing compared to you. You look absolutely beautiful."

Lillian patted the ground next to her. Ruth moseyed over and extended her hand, presenting the bouquet. Lillian graciously accepted, took a big sniff, then placed them on the ground. "They're so lovely, thank you."

Ruth sat next to her, and within no time, they were laughing and eating until the deep sunset colors streaked the sky, and the beginning hint of a full moon appeared low on the horizon. Lillian said they should start gathering everything and head out before it got too dark. Ruth picked up the blanket, and as she folded it, thought now would be the perfect time to kiss Lillian. She couldn't ask for a more romantic backdrop. With her heart pounding and her stomach doing flip-flops, Ruth turned. "Lillian...I—"

Lillian placed a finger on Ruth's lips, stood frozen for a moment, then slowly leaned in. Ruth closed her eyes. Her body was on fire with anticipation and excitement. She could barely contain herself as she waited to feel Lillian's soft, delicate lips. She couldn't count how many times she had played this moment in her head It was the first vision that filled her mind when she woke up and the last one that carried her off to sleep.

The thunder of the horse's hooves was distant, yet audible. Lillian cocked her head.

Ruth slowly opened her eyes, wondering if she'd misread Lillian's motion to kiss her and felt a surge of embarrassment. "Lillian, what's wrong? What is it?"

"I was so careful to cover my tracks. Careful to make sure no one knew." She put a hand over her heart. "It can't possibly be him." She turned.

Ruth registered the fear in her shaking body. "Lillian?" She followed Lillian's line of sight. In the last of the twilight, she saw two men riding through the crops, heading in their direction.

"Run," Lillian screamed. "It's my husband!"

The word hit Ruth like a punch to the gut. Husband? Lillian was married? Stunned, she stared at Lillian, who turned once more and screamed, "Run!"

Ruth spun on her heels and did exactly that.

❖

Ruth's eyes filled with tears. "Lillian yelled at me to run. So I did." She glanced at her boots as she kicked at the dirt. "I didn't know," she mumbled.

"Didn't know what?"

"That she was married." Ruth looked up. "I would have never thought about her like that if I knew she was married. Her husband was one of the two men coming at us. I ran across this land as fast as I could. Back then, it was just an open field. I was so afraid, so very afraid."

"What happened next?"

Tears streamed down her cheeks. "They shot me. Right over there." She pointed to the southeast corner of the vineyard. The same spot Jamie had seen her on full moon nights, sitting with her knees bent, rocking back and forth. "I kept trying to tell them I didn't know, that Lillian never told me. That nothing happened between us. But they killed me anyway."

Jamie let her own tears flow as the shock and injustice gripped her. How could someone murder such a beautiful human being? Hunt her down for no reason and just kill her?

Speechless and riddled with anger, Jamie caressed Ruth's hand. A surge of emotions overtook her. She felt like she was on a rollercoaster as intense fear gripped her body, causing her heart rate to soar, followed by a sharp and painful ache in her shoulder. A second later, she lunged forward, pulled her hand from Ruth's and tried to rub a painful cramp out of her shoulder. What the hell was that? Jamie thought as control over her body and mind returned.

She took a deep breath to calm her heart rate. "How, um… how did my great grandfather play into this?"

"I remember standing over my body, confused. I didn't understand what was going on. It was like being in a foggy state after waking from a dream. I had been lying on the ground, begging for my life, and a blink later, I was standing next to the men who shot me. But no one was saying anything. We all were just standing there, looking down at…me. None of it made any sense, and my mind was so murky at first, it was like I couldn't pull any thoughts into focus.

"When the men finally started talking to each other, without even acknowledging the fact that I was standing next to them, I realized they couldn't see me and that I must really be…dead. I began screaming, and I fell to my knees. I was inches from my own face, staring into eyes that never blinked. Blood was oozing out of my chest and down my shirt. I glanced down at myself. I was wearing the same clothes that I died in, but there was no hole in my chest and no bloodstain on my shirt. I remember thinking that didn't make sense, that nothing was making any sense.

"Then I heard Hank run out of the house and over to us. He greeted the men, and when he asked them what happened, they said I had been messing with the one's wife. They thought like most that I was a simple-minded teenage boy, a life they didn't think twice about putting an end to. But when they checked to see if I was really dead, they discovered I was a woman, and that changed things. Their brief celebration of self-righteous revenge turned to shock and confusion. No one knew what to do. Finally, Hank told them to bury me there. That they could hide their crime because no one would come looking for me here. He brought over shovels, and after they dug the hole, the one man took his boot and rolled me in."

She paused for a moment. "After they buried me, they left without saying a single word of sorrow or remorse. They were ruthless, and I knew I needed to go find Lillian and let her know what had happened. I feared she too was in danger. So I ran as fast as I could. But as soon as I hit the border of the property, I felt excruciating pain, and my body broke into small particles that began mixing with the air and floating away. I remember the sensation of falling into a hole as everything around me started to go black. I fell backward, and when I did, the particles returned and reformed my body. I remember screaming in fear, as I watched my arms rebuild themselves."

She pointed to the southwest corner of the vineyard, "That's where I first tried to leave. Then I tried again from other directions, other angles, other sections of the field. But each attempt ended with the same result. Eventually, I collapsed, curled into a ball, and cried for what seemed like forever. I realized I would never see Lillian again, and that she would never know the truth of what had happened to me."

She looked down. "No one would. When I finally peeled myself off the ground, the two men were gone, and there was no sign of old man Hank. So I began walking the perimeter of the field, trying to figure out and understand the boundaries. I'd reach my arm out and take careful note of when my fingers started to turn into particles. I circled this place over and over again for days until I knew it like the back of my hand. I kept trying to find an opening so I could escape, but I never found one. Eventually, I just kinda accepted the fact that I was stuck. Something that to this day, has been hard to deal with."

"Ruth, I can't even imagine."

"No, I don't suppose anyone could. I can tell you, it's been very hard being stuck on this land. The days and nights are long, and loneliness is a constant companion. At the beginning, I kept thinking I would leave soon, you know, transition to heaven. But nothing's happened, and I don't understand why."

"Are you still buried here?"

"Yeah, like I said, no one knows I'm here, so no one has claimed my remains. I'm, um." She nodded to the southeast corner of the land. "I'm right over there."

Jamie exhaled. "Holy shit. No wonder Great Grandpa Hank drank himself to death. His conscience must have got the best of him. Ruth, I'm so sorry."

"Well, actually, when I figured out I could turn my visibility on and off at will and transport myself small distances around the land, I decided to haunt him."

"You haunted my great-grandpa?"

"I didn't set out to, but I was so mad. Why couldn't people just leave me alone and let me live my life? I guess I took out the anger I had for everyone who hurt me on Hank. I noticed he drank for days after the first time I appeared before him, so I just kept doing it. The more he saw me, the more he drank. I didn't care that it was killing him."

She smiled in a devious way. "I would pour whiskey over him when I found him passed out on the porch and fill his boots with horse droppings, you know, stuff like that. The night I decided to sit in his rocking chair on the porch and strum his banjo while staying invisible was the night he drank himself to death." She gazed at Jamie. "Sorry."

"I don't think I would have been as kind in my hauntings."

❖

Ruth remembered how much her little haunting antics had helped pass the time as the days had turned into months and eventually years. But after Hank's death, she didn't feel right haunting anyone else just for the sake of haunting, so she'd settled back into a state of emotional emptiness.

She still didn't understand why she hadn't transitioned, and the lack of answers combined with being tethered to the land had sent her into a depression. She didn't want to be here, and she most certainly didn't belong here. The few that saw her, feared her, causing her to withdraw even further. She'd stay mostly invisible as she spent her days walking aimlessly around the field with no direction or purpose except to kill the one thing she had plenty of: time. As the years had flipped by, she'd watched the land change hands, stayed to herself, and observed how time changed the world and people around her.

It wasn't until Nora and Kate had taken over that Ruth had finally started enjoying her time again. She was curious about their ways, clothes, language, and sense of unapologetic freedom. And she could tell they were nice decent people, so she remained visible more and more. They had been the first ones to acknowledge her in an inviting and welcoming way. At first, when they would wave to her, she had looked behind her, not believing someone actually viewed her in a positive way. When she'd learned they'd wanted to turn the field into a vineyard, she'd become excited. Her enclosure was maddening at best. Having a change of scenery would be a welcome relief.

With Kate and Nora, Ruth had finally begun to focus on something besides her own pitiful existence. She'd begun to smile and laugh as she'd watched Kate and Nora do the strangest things. Not to mention how their expression of love had made Ruth feel. It was clear that women could now be open about their love for one another. The world beyond this land was definitely marching in the right direction.

"Did you ever see the men who shot you again?"

"No, they never came back here. And I couldn't go after them. Like I said, I can't leave," Ruth whispered.

"So Lillian never knew what had happened to you."

"I'm sure she thought I left town, an easy enough belief, considering." Ruth stood, brushed the dirt from her pants, and helped Jamie up. "Walk with me." She led Jamie over to the southeast corner of the vineyard. "This is where they buried me."

"Ruth, I'm…" Jamie's voice caught as she put her arm around Ruth and pulled her into a tight embrace.

Ruth shivered as Jamie's arms tightened around her. She had no memories of feeling a protective embrace. She'd avoided people in her life and in her death. Intimacy, on the simplest level, was something that had always eluded her. And right now, in Jamie's arms, Ruth understood for the first time what it was like to feel so content with someone that she never wanted to let them go.

When Jamie finally pulled out of the embrace, they stood silently, staring at one another. Jamie placed her hand on Ruth's right cheek and gently stroked with her thumb as Ruth leaned into her hand. "Ruth, I…" Jamie scanned Ruth's face. She leaned in and gave her a gentle kiss, one that seemed to test the waters and with enough pause to give either of them an out if they wanted to take it.

Ruth answered by kissing her back hard and leaving no doubt as to what she wanted. Her body responded, as her kiss deepened. She could feel the sensation of her body pulsing.

Like a heartbeat, after a heavy workout, she could hear the beats echo in her head. When they parted, Ruth pulled Jamie into a warm embrace.

"I'm here for you," Jamie whispered.

Ruth nodded, leaned deeper into Jamie's shoulder and for the first time since her death, sobbed.

❖

Jamie had wondered if Ruth's lips were as soft as they looked. They hadn't been freezing or uncomfortably cold; there was just a chill to them. *I can deal with that.*

She had never felt such a surge of protectiveness as when Ruth was telling her about her death. She hated the men for what they did to her, and she hated Hank for being a part of it. *But how does someone right a wrong that happened over a hundred years ago?* Still, she felt she had to do something for Ruth that marked a life once lived. *No one should ever be forgotten.*

As they walked side by side back to the house, Jamie placed her hand on Ruth's back. A strong feeling of peace settled around her, and Jamie knew in that moment that she was in love.

A plume of dust followed a dark mid-sized maroon SUV as it made its way up the dirt driveway. "Who's that?" Ruth asked. "I don't recognize the car."

"Me neither. Maybe it's Victoria."

"Victoria?"

"Kali's latest love interest. She's an events coordinator. I hope you don't mind, we decided to open up the land and host gay weddings and receptions, so you might be seeing more people around here from time to time."

"Why are you asking if I mind? This is your land."

Jamie turned to Ruth and held both of her hands. "Because this land belongs to you as much as it does me." Jamie looked into her eyes and leaned in to kiss her when she heard a voice that stopped her dead in her tracks.

"Jamie!"

"What?" Ruth pulled away. "What's wrong?"

Jamie shivered as though someone ran their fingernails down a chalkboard. *It couldn't be?*

"Jamie, what is it?"

"*It's* a who, and her name is Cheryl."

CHAPTER FIVE

Jamie walked with an unhurried pace to the front porch. Ruth had vanished as soon as Jamie had said Cheryl's name, and Jamie couldn't blame her. She'd brought Cheryl to the land several times a year when they'd been together, and one time, under an exceptionally bright, star-filled night and after too much wine, she and Cheryl had made love by the firepit. *Ugh.* Jamie cringed. No wonder Ruth vanished. She knew all too well what Cheryl and Jamie once were to each other. But those days were long gone. Now, the only person rocking Jamie's body was Ruth.

Jamie felt a hint of abandonment as she approached the house. It would have been nice to have Ruth by her side right now. Having Ruth vanish at will, leaving Jamie no way of knowing when she would see her again, was not something she thought she could get used to.

Cheryl was sitting on the bench smiling as Jamie shuffled up the steps. A flood of emotions hit her as she looked into Cheryl's eyes. Hate and betrayal mixed with what was once love and attraction. All Cheryl had to do when they were together was flash her baby blues and smile, and Jamie was instantly wrapped around her finger. Add that to a body that was rock solid from hours in the gym and curly blond hair, and it was no wonder Jamie tolerated way more than she should have.

You were once my everything. Damn it, Cheryl. "What are you doing here?"

"I heard about Nora," Cheryl said as she fidgeted. "I know what she meant to you."

"She died over seven months ago." Her voice carried a little more edge than she meant.

"I know. I've, uh, I've kinda been, um, out of the information loop."

"By your own choice." Jamie remembered the feelings of rejection after several attempts to maintain communication with Cheryl failed. Apparently, Jamie wasn't worth the effort of a simple text. It took her months to accept the fact that the woman she had been willing to follow to the ends of the earth no longer wanted anything to do with her.

"Yeah, um, so…the place is yours now, huh?"

"Mine and Kate's." As she leaned against the railing opposite Cheryl, Jamie wondered if her sudden reappearance had more to do with needing money and less to do with a need to deliver condolences. Cheryl's gigs were few and far between and so was her income.

"Those two were inseparable. I'm sorry for Kate. I'm sure she's struggling."

Cheryl's sudden concern was like a punch to the gut after listening to years of her criticizing and poking fun at Kate and

Nora's free-spirited lifestyle. *Like you ever cared.* "Comes and goes, but she's better than she was. Besides, you know Kate. She grieves in her own way."

"Yeah…" Cheryl trailed off as she looked down and began to fidget some more, a sign that she was mulling something over and figuring out a way to say it.

"So, Cheryl, why are you really here?" Only two things motivated Cheryl: attention and money. And since this wasn't the place to come for attention…

Cheryl shifted from her left side to her right and back again. "Well, I um, I wanted to tell you…"

"Oh God, did something happen to your parents?" She hadn't thought about another reason for Cheryl's appearance.

"What? No, no, they're fine. In fact, they just got back from a two-week cruise, and now all they talk about is their latest diet. They want to lose weight so they can go on another cruise and eat themselves into another food coma. Trust me, they're fine."

"Then why are you here?" *Just say it, and stop playing footsie. Begging you for information is such a powerplay.*

"Viv and I broke up."

"Who's Viv?"

"She's my, *was* my girlfriend."

"Oh, sorry to hear that." Jamie tried to calculate what number notch Viv was on Cheryl's belt. The thought disgusted her.

"After we broke up, I took some time to be alone, and I started thinking about us. We were really good together."

Yes, they *had been* good together. They both had the same taste in food, politics, religion, the same sense of humor, and they'd most definitely clicked extremely well in the bedroom. Yeah, *that* part of the relationship had been good. The others, not so much. And that was why Jamie had always felt like she was never Cheryl's primary relationship. She was more like fifth or sixth on the list. Well below liquor, Cheryl's dog, and adoration from strangers. "So let me get this straight, we haven't spoken in over three years, you blocked me from all your social media accounts, you've bounced from girlfriend to girlfriend, and last year, when I reached out and asked to go out for coffee to see if we could have a friendship, you didn't even bother to text me back."

Cheryl stood and sauntered over. "I know I was a shit to you, and I know I fucked up the relationship. But that's not who I am anymore."

Jamie was so stunned that, for a moment, her anger disappeared. For years, she had wanted Cheryl to acknowledge and apologize for her behavior. Instead, Cheryl had painted Jamie as the unstable one in the relationship, the one Cheryl needed to get away from.

"Really?" Jamie snorted.

Cheryl nodded as she reached for Jamie's hands, but Jamie pulled away. "If you give me a second chance, I'll prove to you how happy we can be. I've yet to find anyone like you Jamie. I still love you."

The words hit Jamie like a punch. It had taken her a long time to get over Cheryl. She'd spent way too many days and nights looking into the rear view mirror of their relationship. And even after all the shit she'd gone through, if Cheryl had asked her back in the first year after they'd split, Jamie might have said yes. But the moment she'd rebuilt her self-esteem and self-worth, she vowed she would never again let anyone rob her of who she was.

"Cheryl, I—"

Cheryl leaned in and kissed her.

❖

Ruth stood off to the side, watching the interaction. She remembered when Jamie brought Cheryl on the land. The two had walked hand in hand through the rows of the vines, talking and laughing. And Ruth had never forgotten the night she'd stumbled upon them making love by the firepit. She'd been both embarrassed and aroused. It had been the first time she had ever seen two women making love, and it had been the most beautiful thing she had ever witnessed. Watching Jamie come had made Ruth wish she was the one who'd caused such a beautiful display of pleasure. But she wasn't. And now Cheryl was back, in the flesh, reclaiming Jamie with a kiss.

Ruth knocked a fist against her forehead. *Stupid, stupid, stupid. What were you thinking?* It would never work with Jamie, no matter how much Ruth loved her. Jamie needed a woman who was alive. Someone who could take her to dinner, on vacation, and all the things living people did.

A sickening feeling ripped through Ruth. She wanted to throw up, but she was incapable of the actual act. She fell to her knees as she grieved once again for what had been taken from her on that night so many years ago and what was being taken from her right now. She'd never had a chance to express her love to Lillian, and it was clear she would never have that chance with Jamie. Love was a gift given to others.

With a defeated heart, she stood and forced herself to face the scene unfolding in front of her. She had been robbed of her future, but that didn't mean Jamie should be robbed of hers. She would be doing Jamie a favor by walking away. Jamie needed to live her life free from the complications Ruth would bring.

"Good-bye, Jamie," Ruth whispered through tears. "I will always love you." She turned and walked slowly into the night, until she became one with the darkness.

❖

"Jeezus, Cheryl!" Jamie pushed her away as the mix of hurt and anger surfaced. "You don't get to do that. We're not together." *I am not your pawn. How dare you try to play me?*

"But we could be."

"No, that ship sailed that night you stayed out until two in the morning. Remember? I texted you all night, scared to death something happened to you because you didn't return any of my texts. And when you finally stumbled your drunk ass home, and I asked you where you'd been, you said you didn't owe me an answer because I wasn't your, and I quote, fucking mother. That's why we're not together, Cheryl." The raw anger she thought she'd worked through in therapy came roaring back. "We were done that night."

"Jamie—"

"No."

"But—"

"I said no." She didn't like who she became when she was with Cheryl. A lot of the depression she'd shed after her reunion with Kate and Nora many years ago had settled back in. She'd promised herself to never again live in the dark shadows of life, and yet she had been doing that with Cheryl. "It took me a long time to heal after we broke up. You went on to be with other women. I went to therapy and spent a lot of time reflecting." She inhaled deeply as she tried to calm down, "Look, I'm glad you are taking time to look in the mirror, and I hope you embrace what you see, no matter how uncomfortable it makes you feel."

"You know what, Jamie? I don't need a lecture from *you*," Cheryl snapped.

And there it was, the demon that Jamie had come to know so well. The one who lurked just under the surface, waiting to come out when it heard the wrong thing. "I don't want to fight." She held up her hands.

"Who's fighting? I'm not fighting."

Jamie let out a sigh. Cheryl could have icing all over her face and argue that she was never near the cake. *You're mentally exhausting.* Jamie changed the subject, a survival technique she'd learned a long time ago. When Cheryl's demon reared, the best bet was to steer the conversation down another path. God, she couldn't believe she was living this again. "Look, why don't you come inside, and I'll get you a drink. The place hasn't changed that much since you were last here, but we've made a few improvements."

"No. Thanks, though. I think I'll just head out. I felt the vibe from Kate and Kali when I knocked on the door looking for you. Let's just say it wasn't the most welcoming."

"They just don't want to see me get hurt again."

Cheryl took a step toward her. "I would never hurt—"

"Don't, Cheryl, just don't. You had my heart, and you had your chance. We're just too different. We found that out the hard way, so let's not revisit something we know doesn't work." And with those words, Jamie knew she would never again be manipulated.

"Huh." Cheryl cocked her head as if in thought.

Jamie knew that look well. Cheryl was weighing her odds. She hated to lose and always implemented an exit plan if a situation looked like it might become too embarrassing. "I um, I think I should probably get going. I'm feeling a little weird right now."

No, you're just not used to a woman turning you down. "Come on." Jamie let out a deep sigh. "I'll walk you to your car." *Let's get this disaster of a visit over with.*

Cheryl fell silent as she walked off the porch and over to her SUV.

"New car?" Jamie asked, a bit surprised that Cheryl had replaced her old truck, considering it held a higher place in Cheryl's heart than Jamie.

"New to me. The truck broke down one too many times. I figured it was finally time to get one that started without me saying a prayer every time I put the key in the ignition." She cocked her head. "We had some fun memories in that old truck."

"That we did." Jamie smiled as she opened the door. "It was nice to see you again. Let's do coffee sometime soon, okay?" She knew full well Cheryl would never take her up on the offer. Cheryl would have another "babe" on her arm within a week or two, and Jamie would be bumped back down to pond scum status. Ah, the memories.

Cheryl nodded as she slipped into the car and closed the door. As it skidded forward, it sprayed Jamie in a plume of dust. She coughed as she cleared a layer of dirt from her face and headed to the porch. "You guys can come out now," she said as she spit.

The screen door opened, and Kate and Kali walked out. "What a bitch," Kali said as she shuffled to the bench and sat down.

"How much did you hear?"

"Pretty much the whole thing. We were standing ready in case you needed reinforcements," Kate said as she handed Jamie a glass of wine. "Take a sip, you need it."

"You've perfected your spying technic." Jamie took a sip and swished the welcome liquid around her mouth, then spit it out. The next sip she gratefully swallowed, as well as the gulp after that.

"Finish it off. After that mess of an encounter, you may need the whole bottle." Kate smiled, then said with concern, "Think Ruth saw any of that?"

Ruth! Jamie rubbed her hands over her face. She was sure Ruth had been watching. *Damn it, Cheryl.* She closed her eyes and let out a long sigh. "I need to go find her." She downed the wine, handed the glass back to Kate, and took off down the steps.

"Hey," Kali called.

Jamie turned. "Yeah?"

"You know what they say, sometimes exes come back into your life to see if you're still stupid. I'm glad you passed the test."

"Me too." She snorted as she ran into the vineyard.

CHAPTER SIX

Jamie and Kate moved around the kitchen in total synchronicity. Jamie's mom did not cook, so she had never taught any culinary skills. Taking fast food out of a bag or sticking a frozen meal in the oven had been the extent of her kitchen food prep. It wasn't until she started hanging out at the vineyard that she learned how to cook. Kate would spend hours in the kitchen with her, patiently teaching her about the fine art of cuisine.

Jamie peeled her cell phone out of her back pocket and texted Kali, *Dinner in fifteen.*

"I've never seen her take this much time getting ready." Kate grabbed the package of spaghetti from the cabinet.

"She wants to make an impression." Jamie added a generous pinch of salt to the boiling water.

"All that girl has to do is smile, and she makes an impression."

Jamie chuckled. "That smile has bedded her more women than I care to count."

"I can only imagine."

They both laughed. Jamie dropped the entire package of spaghetti in the water. "I think she really likes this one more than just a one-night stand."

"About time she settled back down."

"Mm-hmm." Jamie moved around Kate, grabbed a wooden spoon and stirred the marinara sauce. She gently brought the spoon to her lips, blew off the excessive heat, and took a taste. "Perfect."

"Still no sign of Ruth?"

Jamie shook her head. It had been three weeks since Cheryl's visit, and Jamie had walked the vineyard every day, calling for Ruth to appear, but she never did. And every evening, she wrapped herself up in a blanket and sat for hours on the bench, hoping beyond hope that Ruth would walk up the steps and join her.

"Ruth?" Jamie had mumbled in a sleepy daze on the tenth night. "You're back?"

"It's just me, sweetie," Kate had said as she'd leaned down and placed an arm around Jamie. "You fell asleep out here."

"What time is it?"

"It's going on midnight. Come on, let's get you to bed."

"No, I want to stay out here another hour or so."

"Tell you what, why don't you go inside and rest on the couch, and I'll sit out here while I finish my wine?"

"No," Jamie had half-heartedly protested.

"Yes. Now come inside."

Jamie had nodded an appreciative *thank you* as she was guided to the couch, where she slept the clock around. When she'd finally woken, Kate had handed her a cup of coffee and had told her it was time to just let things play out with Ruth.

"But what if she stays away for good?"

"Just give her time. She'll come around."

"And if she doesn't?"

"She will."

Jamie clung to the echo of Kate's promise as she stirred the spaghetti.

"I meant to ask you"—Kate draped a towel over her shoulder as she leaned against the counter—"are we having more issues with birds eating the grapes?"

"Not that I'm aware of, why?"

"There're yellow Post-its tied to the vines. I figured you or Kali put them there to scare the birds."

"I did, and they're actually invitations for Ruth to join us for dinner tonight." Jamie placed a pre-sliced baguette on a cookie sheet before placing it in the oven.

"You wrote an invitation on every one of those notes?"

"Yep."

"Wow, nothing obsessive about that at all."

"I'm hoping Ruth—"

Kali burst into the kitchen with her arms outstretched. "How do I look?" she asked as she did a slow twirl. She was barefoot, wearing black jeans, a designer western cut shirt that clung tightly to her muscular frame, and enough gel in her hair to make it windproof.

"You look goddamn sexy, girl, and you know it," Kate said.

"Why, thank you. Hopefully, someone else will concur." Kali strolled to the drawer, took out a tablespoon, and dipped it into the sauce. "Oh man, that's good."

"Yes, it is. Now take your sexy ass out of here while we finish up."

Kali chuckled as she leaned in and kissed her on the cheek.

"Knock, knock?" Victoria's voice called from the front door.

"Gotta love a lesbian who's on time." Kali smiled as she dashed out of the kitchen.

Kate laughed. "She's smitten."

"Mm-hmm," Jamie replied as she strained the spaghetti. "Grab the sauce and the bread."

"Right behind ya."

Jamie walked into the main room and placed the huge bowl of pasta in the middle of the table. Kali and Victoria hadn't made it past the entryway, locked in a passionate kiss. Jamie cleared her throat. "Dinner's served."

Kali peeled her lips off Victoria's, grabbed her hand, and led her to the table. Kate put the sauce and bread down and motioned for everyone to take a seat.

Kali pulled out Victoria's chair. "I'll get the wine."

"Thanks," Jamie called out as she put a ladle in the sauce bowl. For Kali's sake, she wanted tonight's dinner to go well. It was her and Kate's little contribution to what Jamie hoped would be the start of something good for Kali, and it saddened her that Ruth was not by her side enjoying the evening as well.

"Thank you so much for inviting me," Victoria said in a soft voice.

"Well, thanks for coming, Kali's told us a lot about you," Kate said as she sat across from her.

"All good things." Kali leaned over Victoria's right shoulder and poured some wine.

"So, Victoria," Kate said as she sat, "not to put you on the spot or anything, but tell us all about yourself."

"Oh no...that's not putting her on the spot at all," Kali teased as she sat.

"Not really," Victoria smiled at Kali, "that's okay. Well, um, I'm originally from—"

The sound of the screen door creaking interrupted her, and all eyes turned to Ruth, who stood just inside the door. She seemed frozen in place and looked extremely uncomfortable. "I'm sorry if I'm..."

Jamie pushed her chair back and hurried over. Her heart pounded as she touched Ruth's hand and whispered, "Thanks for coming. I was getting worried I'd never see you again."

"I got your notes, all of them, actually. So you really don't want to be with Cheryl?"

"Nope."

"Are you sure?"

"Yes, very much so, I want to be with you."

"But I'm—"

"Perfect. You're perfect, Ruth."

"Well, are we going to have to serve you two over there, or are ya gonna come over here and join us?" Kate said as she ladled sauce on a heaping pile of spaghetti.

Jamie squeezed Ruth's hand. She knew from past conversations that this was the first time Ruth had set foot in the house, and she wanted her to feel welcome. Jamie took a step toward the table, but Ruth jerked back. "There's someone I don't know here. I should go."

"Please don't vanish," Jamie pleaded. "That's Victoria, Ruth, and it's okay, she knows."

"She knows about me?"

"Yes, and it's okay, really. Everyone is anxious to finally meet you." Jamie gently placed her hand behind Ruth's waist and led her to the table. "Everyone, this is Ruth. Ruth, this is—"

"No need. I, um, I know who you are, I've been watching you for years. Nice to finally meet you."

"Likewise, darlin'," Kate said. "Now, don't just stand there. Sit down and join us. You're family here."

❖

"Oh man." Kali pushed back from the table and patted her stomach. "That was seriously good." She reached around Victoria's shoulder, leaned in, and whispered something that elicited a small nod and a big smile. "So, um, I'm going to show Victoria my room and all." They got up and grabbed their plates.

"Nope, put those back down. I've got dishes tonight," Kate said. Tonight, she wanted to handle the cleanup alone. This way Jamie and Kali could enjoy the rest of the evening with Ruth and Victoria, and she could have some time to herself. Having everyone together this evening had triggered thoughts of Nora, and the emptiness had taken hold. "Why don't you go show Victoria your room...*and all.*"

Kali mouthed a thank you as she grabbed Victoria's hand and eagerly led her upstairs, but Kate heard them pause on the steps as she went into the kitchen.

"Ruth looks so real," Victoria said.

"I told you."

"You sure she's really dead?"

"Yep."

"Kinda creepy to think I was talking to a dead person all evening."

"I know, but Jamie's really into her, so we're all kinda going with it. Besides, at least she's not a flesh-hanging-from-bones creepy kind of ghost. It's easier to wrap your head around it all when she looks like she does."

"It's still fucking weird."

"Yeah." They continued upstairs. "But right now, I'm not thinking about Ruth."

Kate smiled as she went back into the main room.

"We won't see them again until tomorrow." Jamie chuckled as she grabbed a small chunk of cheese from the table and flipped it on the floor for Buddy. "There you go, Bud man."

"Buddy used to come say hi to me in the mornings, but I haven't seen him around much lately," Ruth said as Buddy began rubbing their legs, begging for more.

"He doesn't go out much anymore. He mostly just hangs out in here and sleeps." Jamie leaned down and scratched the top of his head. "Turning into an old man, huh, big boy?"

Kate cleared her throat. "So, um, Jamie, why don't you give Ruth a tour of the house?"

"Oh." Jamie turned. "Would you like to see the rest of the house?"

"I'd love to."

Jamie got up and placed her hand under her plate.

Kate gently slapped her hand. "Nope. I said I got dishes tonight, so go on now."

Jamie laughed. "Thanks, Kate."

"Ruth, it was a pleasure to have you join us. I hope you know you are always welcome here."

Ruth nodded. "Thank you, this evening was lovely."

"We aim to please around here," Kate winked as she shooed them off.

Jamie placed a hand on Ruth's shoulder. "Come on. I'll show you around."

As Jamie led Ruth upstairs, Kate gathered more plates and took them into the kitchen. The salvageable food went into containers; the rest was scrapped into the trash. She hummed as she grabbed the bread and set it on the counter. As she opened the drawer that housed the aluminum foil, a chill shivered up her spine as she stared at the longnose lighter sitting off to one side. Clean up can wait, she thought as she placed the bread back on the counter, snatched the lighter, and shoved it in her back pocket. She made her way back into the main room, grabbed her wineglass, and headed for the porch. She continued humming as she opened the screen door and gently closed it behind her.

She bounded down the steps, took a right, and placed her glass on one of the four railroad ties around the firepit. Without breaking stride, she strolled to the storage shed that had sat next to the side of the house. The sliding door stuck a bit, so Kate had to muscle it open. She grabbed three logs off the pile, snagged the bucket of kindling wood, and headed back to the pit. She dumped the contents of the bucket under the stacked logs and set the wood ablaze. She sat on a railroad tie, picked up her wine, and watched the flames roar to life. It was the first fire she had felt like building since they'd spread Nora's ashes in the pit. Prior to tonight, she'd avoided any thoughts of coming out and sitting here. The memories were still too heavy to maneuver around.

"A firepit!" Nora had jumped with excitement the day Kate had revealed the birthday present she'd built one weekend while Nora had been down in Mexico. Kate had thought it would make a romantic place to sit on cool evenings and sip wine or a variety of warm drinks. Little had she known, the pit would soon be their go-to place to eat, dance, discuss life's challenges, or just snuggle under a blanket.

"I miss you, baby," Kate said as she took a gulp and replayed the last night they'd shared together. Nora had lain dying in the medical bed provided by home hospice in the main room of the house. By then, Nora had been sleeping most of the day, her body had been nothing more than skin on bones, and she could only handle sips of fruit juice and small bites of applesauce. She could barely open her eyes, drool had dripped from a mouth she could no longer completely close, and she had lost her ability to stand without help. Late one night, when it had been clear that Nora was reaching the end of her life's story. Kate had lifted her out of bed and had placed her in her wheelchair. She'd skillfully wheeled her down the front porch steps and over to the firepit. Five minutes later, the pit had glowed with a roaring fire.

Kate had gently placed Nora's feet on the ground and had grabbed her hands. "Okay baby, I'm going to lift you up. Ready? One, two…" With a gentle pull, she'd hoisted Nora up until they were face-to-face. She'd leaned Nora's limp body against her own as she'd retrieved a piece of rope from her back pocket and had tied it around their waists. "Okay, now, I'm going to slide my shoes under your feet, okay, babe?"

After a couple attempts, Kate had finally been able to position Nora's feet on top of her shoes. "Good, baby, that's good," she'd said as she'd draped Nora's arms around her shoulders. "Okay…ready?"

With the melody of their favorite song in her head, Kate had begun to hum as she shuffled her feet and gently rocked her body. By the time Kate had finished humming, they had made a complete lap around the pit and back to the wheelchair. "You still got the moves," Kate had choked out through tears.

Nora had opened her eyes for the first time in weeks and had said in a labored breath, "I…always…wanted to go…out dancing."

"I know you did, sweetie, I know," Kate had whispered as she held her in a long embrace, the kind of embrace she'd been scared to let go of because she'd known she was holding on for life, and if she'd let go, her whole world would have gone with it.

"I...love...you," Nora had said. She'd fallen limp and motionless in Kate's arms, never regaining consciousness. She'd passed two days later.

Kate wiped a tear off her cheek as she thought about that night. "Love you forever." She raised her glass to the stars. A huge puff of smoke erupted from the logs, followed by a series of loud crackles and pops.

The flames grew taller and taller until the woman who would always hold Kate's heart danced and twisted as one with the fire. She seemed healthy and vibrant, just as Kate always wanted to remember her.

It was over in a moment, but that was all Kate needed. She jumped up, threw her hands in the air, and started dancing next to the fire, next to her love, next to the thin veil that could never truly separate two hearts. And long after the flames returned to their predictable shape and the image of her lover followed the smoke into the night's sky, Kate danced. *You will always be my beautiful dancing butterfly, and no matter where you are, I promise, when my time is up, I will come find you.*

❖

Jamie slowly led Ruth down the hallway and into her bedroom. A mix of both anticipation and nervousness surged through her as she closed the door behind them. Fanaticizing about making love to Ruth was one thing; the reality of actually doing it was scaring the shit out of her.

"What a beautiful room," Ruth whispered as she glanced around.

The set of oak furniture was tastefully arranged around a queen-size platform bed. Abstract paintings of topless women in various poses graced the walls.

"A friend of mine in Phoenix painted those."

"They're beautiful." Ruth ran her fingers over the canvas. Jamie put her arms around Ruth's waist, and Ruth leaned into the embrace and sighed. "I was born at the wrong time."

"A lot has changed, that's for sure."

Ruth nodded and turned. Jamie gazed at her. They had already tested the waters of desire, and permission had already been granted. It was time to act on it. Jamie leaned in and kissed Ruth deeply. Ruth's moan put Jamie in motion, and she guided Ruth to the bed. She maneuvered her onto her back and crawled on top of her. "You okay with this?"

"I've been waiting my entire life and all my death for a moment like this. I think I'm more than ready."

A slap of reality hit Jamie when she heard the word death. She had only seen Ruth's face and arms. What would the rest of her look like?

Ruth must have sensed Jamie's sudden hesitation. She caressed her face. "Jamie?"

"I, uh, your clothes, do they come off?"

Ruth began unbuttoning her shirt, exposing flawless flesh. "Yes, I can remove them, but oddly, after about a half hour, I become fully dressed again, always in this exact outfit."

"Why?" After that amount of time, did her entire body turned into something else that had to be covered up? Jamie shivered at the thought but quickly put it on hold as Ruth peeled the shirt from her body, exposing small breasts with hard, rosy nipples. Her body was lean and muscular, evidence of the physical labor she had been doing at the time of her death. *Damn, she's beautiful.*

"I don't know why." Ruth lowered her head. "I don't know much. I've had so many questions but never anyone to ask." Ruth glanced up at her. "I've even shouted at the sky and screamed, why me? Why this? But I never get a reply. After a while, I stopped asking. I had felt abandoned so many times in my life. Why should my death be any different?"

Jamie's heart filled with sympathy for someone who'd lived a life so devoid of love and happiness. "Ruth, I..." Sympathy turned to desire as Jamie cupped her face and kissed her deeply. At that moment, it wasn't about the earthly definition of life. It was about the laws of attraction and the energy that was being exchanged between two souls connecting.

Jamie broke from the kiss. "If I do anything that makes you feel uncomfortable or—"

Ruth put a finger on her lips. "Shh, you're talking too much."

Jamie smiled as she pressed into Ruth, who responded by kissing her hard and long. Jamie kept her lips against Ruth's as she mumbled, "Clothes off now."

Ruth nodded as Jamie rolled off her, and in a dance of synchronicity, both striped the rest of their clothes off. Jamie rolled back on top of Ruth and took a moment to glance at her body. Although it lacked the subtle movement in the stomach when a breath was taken, Ruth's body was as real as her own. And right now, all she wanted to do was touch it, kiss it, suck it.

"Ruth, I want to…"

"Again, talking too much."

Jamie felt a warm and very wet sensation between her legs as her body signaled its desire to be touched. She kissed Ruth hard, extending her tongue into Ruth's mouth, searching and finally wrapping around Ruth's. Jamie moaned from somewhere deep inside, as she broke the kiss and licked her way down Ruth's neck to then circle over her breast. Ruth arched as Jamie playfully bit her nipple.

Jamie's own body responded. Her nipples became so erect, a surge of painful pleasure emerged from them. She took her mouth off Ruth's nipple as she let out a breath. *Holy fuck, that was intense.* Her body had never responded like that before. Every nerve ending was releasing mini shocks throughout her body.

"Is everything okay?" Ruth whispered.

Jamie's arousal heightened, and her need to release the energy building inside her became more urgent. "More than okay," she whispered as she leaned in to continue what she'd started. As soon as she returned to Ruth's nipple, a strong tingle went through her, and a feeling of intoxication took hold. Strong arousal played out as she caressed every inch of Ruth's body. Ruth in turn gave back what she was receiving.

The lines of lovemaking blurred as the energy they shared began merging as one. Their bodies danced in tandem as the sensation of giving and receiving became impossible to distinguish. When Jamie finally entered Ruth, she felt the full sensation of Ruth's fingers moving inside her, harder and faster, until Jamie came as intensely as Ruth did. They were one, desire matching desire.

Afterward, as they lay naked in each other's arms, Jamie wasn't sure what had hit her. She had never experienced lovemaking of that caliber. Or an orgasm with such intensity.

"Thank you," Ruth said in a soft voice, "for giving me such a beautiful gift."

"I can say the same."

"Jamie?" Ruth said as she placed her head on Jamie's shoulder and spooned her.

Jamie kissed the top of Ruth's head. "Hmm?"

"I finally know what love is."

Jamie's heart melted. She closed her eyes and thought of everything that had happened in her life that had led to this moment. How was it possible that two women from different dimensions could fit so perfectly together? Ruth was Jamie's forever. She felt it deep within her bones, and a sadness crept up as she thought about the day her body would eventually succumb to the decline of age, and she would have to leave Ruth. Would they be together in eternity? *Is anybody together in eternity?*

Ruth seemed to lack the reassurances that Jamie craved about the afterlife. The knowledge that, in the end, everything would be okay. *My little ghost who fell through the cracks.* Jamie chuckled to herself. She kissed Ruth's head a second time and reminded herself to cherish every moment of life that they would spend together. Anything beyond that was anyone's guess. "I love you, Ruth," Jamie said as she pulled the covers over them. And although Ruth didn't reply, the blue light pulsing below the sheet said it all.

CHAPTER SEVEN

Jamie watched six hired hands move in a synchronized swarm as they placed bouquets on five, large, round banquet tables covered in lavender tablecloths. Long strands of white LED lights, strung overhead from temporary poles, provided the perfect amount of romantic ambient light.

Three rows of chairs, placed far enough apart for two people to walk between them, sat five chairs deep. And two wedding photographers were already capturing the many memories that would soon grace albums and social media.

Jamie went to stand by Kali and Victoria.

"Shit." Kali raked her fingers through her hair as she glanced at her phone. "Vic?"

"What is it?" Jamie asked.

"Hold that thought," Victoria said as she called out to a fifty-something woman with a hard-shell guitar case strapped to her back. "Set your mic and equipment up over there." She pointed to an empty white folding chair that sat to the left of an eight-foot wedding arch graced with a variety of beautiful white flowers woven into the structure. "Okay." Victoria turned back to Kali. "What's up?"

"Annie's running about twenty minutes behind. Her van had a flat tire, so she's just now heading out."

"Shit," Victoria repeated as she closed her eyes and rubbed her temples. "Okay…that's okay, um, we'll just have Tammy stretch the ceremony a bit. Could you go make sure Linda has everything she needs?"

"Linda is the…" Jamie said as Kali moved off.

"Musician."

"Ah, yes. Got it. I'll go tell Tammy." Jamie hopped up the porch steps and flung open the screen door.

People moved in and out of multiple room dividers erected in haphazard patterns, creating a private dressing room and staging area. A twenty-something makeup artist with pink-streaked hair fluttered in and out of the dividers, tending to the anxious brides and a handful of bridesmaids. Jamie scanned the room until she spotted Tammy on the corner of the couch, which had been pushed flush against the far wall along with the coffee table and TV stand.

"Tammy," Jamie said as she maneuvered through the sea of people and plopped next to her. "The caterer's running about twenty minutes behind. Can you stretch the ceremony speech a bit?"

Tammy took a moment to finish chewing on a piece of cheese before confidently nodding. "Sure, I can do that."

"Great." Jamie got up again and pushed through the new screen door and took a moment to appreciate its silence. Although the old one had character, the new one, according to the salesman at the home construction warehouse, had an automatic hydraulic close feature that promised to be as quiet as a whisper and a metal screen that kept out both bugs and burglars.

She checked the countdown clock on her phone for the umpteenth time. The wedding would begin in exactly one hour, three minutes, and forty-two seconds. Right at sunset as the brides requested. If all went as planned, the vows would be spoken as nature painted the sky with a palette of reds, oranges, and yellows. And by the time the guests finished their dinner, their backdrop would be a beautiful full moon. Jamie said another thank you to the weather gods for making the evening, according to her weather app, *cloudless with a slight breeze out of the southwest that would cool the evening to a pleasant seventy degrees.* The pictures would be the debut photos for their website and Legacy's. Jamie wanted the vineyard to be picture perfect to help lure the many bookings she hoped would follow this one. And from the way the evening was shaping up, the vineyard would be a desired venue for many more weddings and receptions.

"Hey, Kal," Jamie said as she approached.

Kali grunted.

"You look as fidgety as the brides." Jamie placed her hands on Kali's shoulders and tried to massage away the tension. "The place looks beautiful, and the weather is perfect. Relax."

"I just want everything to go right, you know?"

"It will. Your girlfriend is an incredible coordinator. She's got this."

"She is amazing, huh?"

"Yep, she's a keeper." Jamie hoped Kali registered the subtle hint in her reply and that she'd think twice before discarding this one. Victoria seemed grounded. The perfect Yin to Kali's Yang.

Jamie took a moment to admire the transformation of the vineyard. After they'd signed the contract with Legacy, they'd decided to max out the company credit card, taking a gamble that the money from their upcoming harvest added to their wedding venue fee would repay the debt and then some. Plus, as Kate had not so subtlety reminded her, it was an investment in their future wedding business. A business they could hopefully rely on throughout the year, offsetting the times mother nature wasn't so kind. With constant threats of too little rain, too much rain, frost, fungus, and pests, weddings would definitely be the safer bet.

The first of the renovations had started two weeks ago, when they'd grated the dirt driveway and all the land surrounding the house and Ginger's barn. They had a light gray gravel spread two inches thick over the driveway and to the right of the barn, large enough to accommodate dozens of cars. Since the section around the house would be the staging area for weddings, they chose to pave it with oversized red patio bricks, making it easy for people to walk and dance in dress shoes without worrying about twisting an ankle.

Kali's phone chimed, and she almost dropped it as she fumbled it from her back pocket. "Vic needs more bottled water in the staging area now."

"There's six full cases in the kitchen. I'll go."

"I got it. You stay out here." Kali turned and made a dash for the house without waiting for a reply.

A shiver made its way up Jamie's spine as she smiled. Ever since she and Ruth had made love, Jamie could sense Ruth's energy before she materialized. "Hello, my beautiful ghost," she said in a soft voice as she turned.

"Hello, my beautiful human." Ruth gave Jamie a long kiss that sent tingles down Jamie's body and ended with moisture between her legs.

"Keep that up and I'm going to walk funny until my underwear dries."

"Jamie." Ruth playfully slapped Jamie's arm as her skin pulsed blue. Jamie grabbed her forearm and ushered her to the side of the house. "Sorry, there're times when I just can't help it."

"I know, sweetie, and you know I love it when you pulse," Jamie whispered as she nibbled on her ear. Jamie had noticed that Ruth had been pulsing a lot lately. She had told Jamie it was from the excitement over seeing two women getting married. For that exact reason, Jamie thought it would be best if Ruth remained in the shadows during both setup and ceremony. No sense drawing unwanted questions and unwanted attention about the vineyard's special resident. Like Nora had before her, Jamie never wanted to turn Ruth into a spectacle for people's interest and entertainment. Jamie couldn't imagine anyone in life or death wanting that type of overblown attention.

Ruth leaned into Jamie's arms. "Victoria has done a remarkable job with everything. I really like her."

"Yes, she has, and I like her too. But I can already sense Kali becoming a bit unsettled with her."

"Why? She's lovely?"

"My guess is that Kali's feeling emotions she hasn't felt in a long time, and it's really scaring her. Kali always likes to leave the door cracked open for a fast escape. I blame that on Cruella."

"Cruella?"

"It's the name Kali gave her ex. She used to call her, she who shall not be named, but that was too long, so she shortened it to Cruella. It's the name of a cartoon character who was particularly despicable. She used to constantly tell Kali that she wasn't good enough."

"But that's nonsense. Kali's quite charming."

"Yes, she is, but of all the voices Kali hears in her head, that's the one she chooses to listen to."

"How horrible."

"Yeah, well, hopefully, she'll work through it soon because if she pushes Vic away, I think she'll regret it." *And I'll end up spending the next six months sitting up with her as she cries over it.* Jamie knew that no matter what, she would always be there for Kali. But watching her go from girlfriend to girlfriend was starting to get old. *You can only watch someone self-destruct so many times before it starts draining your own energy.*

Jamie's phone chimed, and she glanced at the screen. She twisted her upper body just enough so the text was out of Ruth's sight.

"That Kali?" Ruth said with a hint of suspicion.

"Uh, no actually, it's a uh, a vendor. Wanting to know what time tomorrow they should come by and get their tables and chairs." She finished her text, shoved her phone in her back pocket, leaned in and kissed Ruth. She was lying to Ruth, and part of her sensed that Ruth knew it. But she couldn't help it. She had started something in secret that she needed to finish. Just one more day, Jamie thought as a touch of excitement surged through her, just one more day.

❖

"Ladies." Kate came over and stood beside Ruth and Jamie as they leaned against the house.

"How's Ginger?" Ruth asked as she thought of the day Kate had first brought Ginger to the property.

"Fed, kissed, and tucked in for the night."

Ruth had bonded with Ginger immediately. She had been broken both physically and mentally from an abusive human with a soulless heart. Every time Ruth placed a hand on Ginger, she could feel her tired soul. "I know the feeling, old girl," Ruth would softly say to her as she sat in the stall night after night, keeping Ginger company.

When Ruth had been eight, her dad would swing her up on his horse, Roamy, and lead him in a big circle around their backyard while Ruth had squealed with delight. Sadly, it was the only happy memory she had of her father. She made it a point to thank Ginger every day for reminding her of the only time in her childhood when she'd truly felt the definition of pure joy. "We'll heal each other," Ruth had promised Ginger. "We have to."

"How's it going out here?" Kate asked.

"So far so good." Jamie trailed off as Victoria came bounding out of the house and headed for the musician.

"I'll need you to start playing in fifteen minutes," Victoria shouted.

The musician nodded as she tuned her guitar.

"Looks like it's showtime." Kate patted Ruth's and Jamie's shoulders as a white van raced up the driveway.

"I think that's Annie." Jamie pulled her phone out.

Ruth turned to her. "I'll check in with you later. For now, I'll get out of everyone's way."

❖

"You're not in—" But before Jamie could reassure her, Ruth vanished.

Kate chuckled. "Damn, I'm in awe every time she does that."

"Yeah, she's pretty amazing." The more Jamie was around Ruth, the more she admired her. For all she had been through, Ruth maintained a kindness that Jamie herself didn't think she would be capable of if she had experienced even half of what Ruth had.

Kali bolted out of the house. "Jamie, Kate, Vic, help me unload Annie's van." She pointed to a spot close to the barn where two long banquet tables were set up.

Annie rushed out the van door and rounded the back. "Sorry Kali, sorry," she said as she handed chafing dishes to outstretched hands.

"It's all good. The ceremony hasn't started yet," Kali said.

"Of all times to get a flat."

"No worries, Annie, we'll get you going before the brides take one step out of the house."

They set up the banquet table in record time. Plates and desserts bookended an assortment of delicious smelling pastas, breads, veggies, and sauces. After a few adjustments, Annie lit the gel burners and signaled with a thumbs-up that she was ready to go.

Victoria's phone chimed. "It's time." She ran in the house and announced to the wedding party that it was time to begin the ceremony.

Perfectly tuned strings vibrated chord after cord as Linda's alto voice sang a folk song about the love between two people and marking the beginning of the ceremony. A hushed audience of family and friends turned as Tammy walked up the aisle and took her place under the floral archway. Six bridesmaids followed in single file, each wearing a short dress that represented one of the colors of the rainbow. When they reached Tammy, the first three veered off to her right, the remaining three to her left.

As Linda seamlessly transitioned into an acoustic version of "Hallelujah," Leslie and Wendy walked hand in hand up the aisle. Both were beautiful Latinas in their mid-thirties, with long, perfectly styled hair and curvy bodies. They both wore white dresses that had a casual and simple design.

They had been together for over five years, and Jamie had liked them from the moment she'd met them. As she watched each look in the other's eye and shed tears of joy, she said a prayer, hoping their union wouldn't end in a statistic.

Jamie felt hands wrap around her waist, and she leaned back into Ruth. "Think that'll ever be us?" Ruth asked.

"Would you like it to be?"

"Yes," Ruth whispered. "I would like to think there's a reason I'm still around."

Jamie turned and kissed her passionately as Tammy finished a heartfelt speech about the freedom to love whoever you chose and announced, "You are now together in love and life until death do you part."

Cell phones were held high as the sunset glowed with vibrant golden light. This was the moment everyone had been waiting for. The moment when Leslie turned to Wendy, leaned in, and kissed her at the exact moment the sunset splashed its colors across the sky.

Jamie knew this picture would be the vineyard's main photo on the Legacy website. Every aspect of their hard work had led up to this moment. This would be the perfect postcard representation of the vineyard for all future weddings to come.

But as their lips were about to touch, Buddy sauntered in from out of nowhere, flopped by their feet, hiked his back leg, and started cleaning his private parts.

Jamie started to run in and remove him, but the laughter and good cheer put her at ease. Wendy even bent and started petting him, and he flopped on his back and rolled from side to side.

Jamie cringed. "Well, that'll be the social media shot we weren't hoping for."

As the brides made their way back down the aisle, Linda announced, "Everyone, please take advantage of the open bar and help yourselves to the wonderful assortment of food. The dancing will begin after the chairs are cleared, and the brides wanted me to assure you that all of your favorite music suggestions are loaded into their dance music mix. Congratulations again to Leslie and Wendy."

A round of applause erupted as family and friends slowly made their way to both the bar and food. Linda sang a short set that lasted through dinner, then signed off as digital music was piped through the speakers, prompting people to get up and dance. Five songs in, a slow melody began, and Kali grabbed Victoria's hand and escorted her to the floor. The full moon sat low on the horizon, and between that and the sunset ceremony, the vineyard delivered as a place to celebrate the uniting of love.

Jamie couldn't help feel the irony. Ruth was murdered on this land because of who she had loved, and now it stood as a place to celebrate that same form of expression.

❖

"You used to play at Rainbows Edge, didn't you?" Kate smiled at the distant memories as she approached Linda, who was standing by the banquet table spooning sauce over her plate of pasta.

"I did."

"I thought I recognized you. My partner and I used to go there from time to time. Too bad it closed." Kate grabbed a plate and placed a sourdough roll on the edge.

"Yeah, the owner wasn't putting much love into the place before she retired, so it just kinda fizzled out. I'm Linda, by the way."

"Kate. Nice to meet you." Kate shook her hand and smiled at the memories Linda's presence sparked.

"Did you guys ever go on theme nights?"

"Are you kidding, practically every one. Our favorite was the one where you had to dress as a cartoon character."

"I didn't go to that one, but I heard there was a great turnout."

Kate nodded as she thought of her and Nora on the dance floor, dressed as Batman and Robin. It had been one of the rare times they'd stayed until the bar announced last call. When they'd finally said their good-byes to friends and had shuffled to their car, Nora had wrapped Kate in her Batman cape and kissed her. "We made a great team in there tonight."

"We're the dynamic duo, of course we made a great team. Besides, where would Robin be without her Batman?"

Missing you with all her heart, that's where Robin would be. "I, um, yes…there was a great turnout on those nights."

"Which bride are you here for?" Linda dipped her roll into the sauce and took a bite.

"Oh, I um, I live here."

"You live here? Wow, I'm impressed."

"Well, thank you."

"This place is gorgeous."

"Thanks, a lot of hard work and love has been poured into this land."

"I bet. Is it just you and your girlfriend?"

"Not anymore. She passed away not quite a year ago. I co-own the place with her niece. Kali"—Kate pointed to the dance floor—"lives here too. She's my niece's best friend."

"I'm so sorry about your girlfriend. It does get better, but it's a slow crawl at times. My wife passed away three years ago. She, um, she was murdered."

Kate about choked on a bite of food. "Murdered?"

"Yeah, shot in her office building along with seven others from a disgruntled employee."

"That's got to be…" Nora's death had felt like a punch to the gut, and Kate had time to prepare and say good-bye. She couldn't imagine being deprived of that gift.

"Insanely impossible to process. Yes, it is." Linda looked down then turned to her. "Say, um…would you like to grab some coffee sometime?"

"Oh, I'm not interested, but thank you."

"No, no, not like that. I just thought, you know, since we both lost our lovers, maybe it would be nice to talk with someone who knows what it's like to feel the…"

"Emptiness?" Kate regarded her. "You know, on second thought, I think getting together for coffee would be nice."

Linda pulled out a Velcro sports wallet and a business card. "My cell number's on the back. Let me know what date works for you."

Kate took the card as she thought of Nora. "Thanks, I will." *Calm down, I'm not cheating on you, baby, it's just coffee. You know you're the only one who will ever have my heart.*

"Linda, come join us!" Wendy waved as a group of people started forming a dance train.

"Looks like the human train needs a caboose. I hope to see you around."

Kate slid the card in her back pocket and thought it would actually be nice to talk to someone who understood the magnitude of loss on that level. Kate finished the last bite of her roll and began to dig into the pasta as she walked away. The conversation with Linda had triggered her loneliness, and she decided to talk it out with Ginger.

As Kate pulled open the barn door and headed for Ginger's stall, she wished again that Nora's soul was on this land like Ruth's. She missed Nora's smile, her free spirit, and her love of life. *Where'd you go, baby? And wherever you are, will I ever see you again?* Her eyes watered as she stroked Ginger's face. "Maybe it's about time to get you a companion, huh, sweetie? No sense both of us being lonely."

❖

It was after midnight before the red taillights of the last car pulled down the driveway, signaling the end of a successful first wedding. Jamie arched her back, trying to work out the stiffness as she followed the others into the house. Victoria and Kali scooted the couch away from the wall and back where it belonged as Kate waved Jamie over to help her put the coffee table and TV stand back in place.

"These cookies are amazing," Ruth said as she walked out of the kitchen holding a half-eaten chocolate chip cookie in one hand and a plastic container full of two dozen more in the other. She was pulsing blue and blinking from invisible to solid like a strobe light.

"Holy shit, Ruth, those are my pot cookies. How many have you had?" Kate hurried over, grabbed the container, and sifted through the contents as she walked to the couch.

"Oh, I don't know, maybe one or seven. Did anyone ever tell you your shirt is the most beautiful color?"

Jamie gently grabbed her hand to lead her to the couch. "You okay, babe? You're kinda doing something I've never seen you do before."

"You've never seen me eat a cookie?"

"What? No, I've seen you eat lots of cookies. I'm talking about the blinking thing you've got going on."

Ruth glanced at Jamie and blinked her eyes in an exaggerated way. "Like this?"

"Happy now?" Jamie shuffled Ruth past Kate and settled her on the couch. "You got my girlfriend stoned."

"I wrote Cannabis Cookies on the lid." Kate put the container on the coffee table, and Vic and Kali both reached over and took one.

Jamie huffed. "Ruth doesn't know what cannabis means."

"She does now." Kali chuckled as she took a bite. "Wow, these are really good Kate."

"Yes, they are," Ruth reached into the container, but Jamie took the cookie and put it back. "I think that's enough for one night."

Ruth giggled as she turned to Jamie. "Sweetie, did you know you have purple hair?"

Victoria and Kali burst out laughing as Kate lowered her head to hide her smile. Jamie picked up a cookie and playfully threw it at Kate. "I'm pawning her off on you tonight if those cookies have some weird effect on ghosts."

Kate had perfected the art of baking with cannabis when one of the side-effects of Nora's treatments was loss of appetite. And although the baked goods were a godsend for Nora, and for Jamie and Kali when life seemed to get the best of them, right now, Jamie was too tired to deal with any negative side-effects the cookies might have on Ruth.

"What? She'll be fine." Kate said. "Won't you, Ruth?"

Ruth make the okay sign, then slowly wiggled her fingers as if fascinated with their movement. Even Jamie couldn't help but laugh.

Kali stood. "Oh, hey, I almost forgot. Everyone, stay here. I've got a bottle to show you. Be right back." She shoved the rest of her cookie in her mouth and bounded up the stairs.

Kate turned to Jamie. "This better not have anything to do with a tampon."

Jamie laughed and pinched the bridge of her nose. "You just had to bring that visual up again." Jamie chuckled to herself at the cringeworthy memory, then smiled as her mind drifted to seeing Ruth for the first time that same evening. She grabbed Ruth's hand and gently squeezed. *Life sure is full of beautiful surprises.*

A minute later, Kali was back down with her hands behind her back. She paused as if for dramatic effect, then brought her hands forward. In each was a bottle of merlot with their new logo on it. "Welcome to Four Friends wine."

"Kali, where did you get these?" Jamie asked.

"I had Chanadoah run a case. What do you think?"

Jamie took one of the bottles and ran her fingers over the label. An ink drawing showed their vineyard in the foreground, the Victorian house in the background, and behind the script font that spelled out Four Friends was the hint of a full moon. It was classy and elegant. "It's beautiful Kali." She thought about the last few years as she'd watched Kate struggled with the needs of both Nora and the vineyard. Both in decline and both requiring attention.

A twinge of guilt came over her. She wished she would have been there more for Kate. But she had been too caught up in her job and her post-relationship depression to understand what Kate had been going through. *I was so selfish. Kate deserves more of the land ownership than I do.*

Jamie continued to stare at the label. The land was still in need of tender loving care, but the prospect of many more weddings on the horizon would mean the vineyard was going to survive. And holding a bottle of wine with their label on it made the journey real and definitely worth it. *Nora would be proud.*

Kate popped the corks as Jamie grabbed the glasses. "A toast," Kate announced as she raised her glass. "To a successful first wedding. May there be many more."

"And to Victoria, who coordinated the hell out of today. You were amazing." Jamie tilted her glass.

"I'll second that." Kali leaned in and gave Victoria a passionate kiss.

Kate hopped up and grabbed what was left of the cheese and crackers. They continued to drink, nibble, and talk for thirty minutes, and Kali and Victoria excused themselves through yawns and made their way up the stairs.

"Come on, my stoned ghost, time for bed. I'm beat." Jamie stood, pulled Ruth off the couch, and turned to Kate. "You coming up?"

"Not yet. I think I'll watch a little TV and relax a bit more. Throw me that blanket, would you?" She pointed to the soft green fleece hanging on the back of one of the cushions. In one motion, Jamie grabbed the blanket and flung it across the coffee table. Kate pulled off her boots and spread the blanket over her legs as Buddy jumped on her lap and settled in.

"Night, Kate." Jamie waved as she headed up the stairs with Ruth. "I take it you've never been stoned before?"

"Stoned? No, no one's ever stoned me. Why?"

Jamie shook her head and pinched the bridge of her nose as they rounded the top of the stairs and headed to her bedroom. "Come on, you, let's hope this wears off soon." *If not, I'm going to kill Kate.*

❖

Kate grabbed the remote and hit the power button. She flipped through several options until she settled on an old romantic comedy. She reached in her back pocket and retrieved her phone as well as the business card that Linda had given her and thought about Nora as she nestled into the cushion, remembering one day in particular.

"I think we should get married." Kate put her arms around Nora, who was placing a cookie sheet with several slices of day-old pizza in the oven. She hummed as she moved her hips to a slow song that she hoped Nora would recognize. Nora closed the oven door, flipped the dial to high broiler, then turned and kissed Kate deeply as they peeled away from the range, and the kitchen became a dance floor.

"Married, huh?"

"Yep."

"And you think dancing sexy with me in the kitchen will seduce me into walking down the aisle with you?"

"That and what I'm going to do to you after dinner."

"Well, how could a woman turn down an offer like that?"

"She can't." Kate leaned into Nora's shoulder. She loved the way their bodies fit together like two halves coming together to make a whole. "I was thinking about asking Jane to design silver bands for us. Maybe with a grapevine etched around the ring."

"A woman after my own heart." Nora kissed her long and hard. "Keep that up and...shit!" Smoke billowed from the oven. Nora lunged for the oven door and opened it as a plume of smoke rose, setting off the smoke detector. She grabbed the kitchen towel and pulled the cookie sheet of charred pizza out of the oven and threw it into the sink as Kate spastically moved her arms in a desperate attempt to clear the air.

"What are you doing? Is there a bug in here?"

"What?" Kate said loudly over the alarm as she continued her motion.

Nora started laughing so hard, she bent over and placed her hands on her knees. A moment later, the alarm stopped going off.

"What?" Kate said as she joined in the laughter.

"I couldn't tell if you're chasing away a bug or trying out some crazy new dance moves."

"I was trying to clear the air," Kate said between a gut-wrenching laugh that was sending tears down her cheek. It was one of the things she loved about Nora. One minute they could be intimately engaged, and the next, they were laughing their asses off. Never a dull moment and never a dull life.

"Oh, is that what you call something like...ouch." Nora grabbed at her left side.

"What is it, babe?" Kate's laughter turned to concern.

"Oh, I've been having these sharp pains in my side and lower back lately. I'm sure it's nothing."

"Well." Kate pulled Nora up and moved her close. "Maybe it wouldn't hurt to make an appointment with the doctor. Wouldn't want anything happening to the future Mrs. Spalding."

Nora gave her a reassuring kiss. "There isn't a force strong enough in nature to prevent that from happening."

"Apparently, there was," Kate said in a soft voice as she replayed the memory while sipping her wine. As the visual in her head faded, and she refocused on the room, she picked up her phone, opened her email app, and typed a note to Jane.

Hey Jane,

I was thinking. I'd like to go ahead and order the wedding band I talked to you about before Nora passed. Same design with the etched grape leaf, but obviously, just make one.

Call when you can.

Kate

Kate tossed her phone on the coffee table, leaned her head back, and let the exhaustion of the day blur her vision as she tried to focus on the TV. Minutes later, her head tilted to the side, and the characters on the TV morphed into the ones dancing in her dreams.

❖

Ruth announced her presence by clearing her throat as she slowly walked up behind Kate, rounded the couch, and sat beside her.

Kate jerked awake and rubbed at her eyes. "Everything okay, Ruth?"

"Yep, just one of the side effects of being dead…you never sleep. Jamie, however, fell asleep immediately. I usually wait until she's in a deep sleep before I vanish and walk around the vineyard, visit Ginger, or come down here and hang out with Buddy. I hope I'm not intruding on your space. I saw the glow of the TV, so I decided to see if you were still awake. Why are *you* still up after such a long day? And can I have another cookie?" Ruth rambled in one quick breath as she scooted closer to Kate and stared at the container of cookies.

"One more but don't tell Jamie I gave it to you. I think we'll save the rest for later, okay?"

Ruth nodded as she bit into a cookie. "I feel so strange right now but in a good way."

"I can tell." Kate chuckled as Ruth continued to pulse and blink.

Ruth finished off the cookie in three bites. "Really, why are you up?"

"I think I fell asleep for a few minutes right before you came down."

"Oh, I'm sorry."

Kate waved her off. "Don't be, I'm usually up watching TV until the wee hours of the morning. It helps me process through stuff better when the house is quiet, and everyone's asleep."

Ruth was well aware of Kate's late-night schedule. She had seen her sitting on the porch many nights, sipping wine and crying. It was moments like those that Ruth wanted to approach and say how much she'd loved Nora, how much she'd loved them both and how much she wished she had someone like them in her life when she was alive. She regretted never taking Nora up on her many invitations to connect and communicate.

It was because of Nora and Kate that Ruth had started to shed the anger and bitterness she'd held on to since her death. Watching their love grow through the years had not only warmed her heart, it reminded her that not everyone had a dark soul.

A shameful twinge shot through her. She should have approached Kate after Nora died and extended her condolences. Kindness should have followed kindness. Instead, it had taken a back seat to her fear and insecurities. "Kate, I…" She noticed Linda's card sitting on the coffee table and changed the course of her thought. Was Kate thinking of venturing out? "Linda seemed nice."

Kate smiled. "I thought so too."

"Did she ask you out?"

"She did. For coffee but it's not what you think."

"Oh?"

"Her lover was killed in an office shooting. We're going for coffee to kinda talk through the feelings of losing a partner."

"Oh, how horrible." Ruth frowned and wondered what kind of reaction Lillian would have had if she'd known Ruth had been shot.

"I know. I can't even imagine. At least I was able to say good-bye to Nora."

Ruth regarded her. "Um."

"Hmm?"

"I'm really sorry I didn't approach you after Nora died. I wanted to, I just, oh, I don't know. I figured I'd probably scare you off or something. But watching your love for each other all these years is what gave me the courage to approach Jamie. I once overheard Nora say, the heart is a muscle—"

"Don't let it atrophy," Kate finished and smiled. She took Ruth's hand. "Thank you, and for the record, not much scares me these days."

Ruth nodded and leaned her head on Kate's shoulder. How she wished she'd had a mother like Kate. Kind, caring, and so full of love. Kate repositioned the blanket so half the fabric covered Ruth.

Ruth was about to tell her not to bother—temperatures no longer affected her—but in that moment, she realized the gesture wasn't about that. The gesture was about showing Ruth she was one of them now. She had a place to call home and people who loved and cared about her. Ruth smiled and snuggled under the blanket as they both turned to the TV and watched in comfortable silence until Kate fell asleep again.

Ruth slowly leaned forward, careful not to wake Kate as she reached for her new favorite cookies. She bit into the soft gooey sweetness and wondered why they made her feel so different. Cookies had changed a lot over the past one hundred years. Ruth settled into the cushion and laughed at the strange characters on the screen, who were dressed in tight outfits and capes while performing unrealistic stunts. She marveled again at the devices that entertained people these days and giggled at the silliness that sometimes came with them. One thing was for sure, she couldn't remember a time when she'd felt so light and happy...and so interested in food.

CHAPTER EIGHT

The smell of freshly ground coffee and pancakes filled the house, enticing Jamie as she shuffled into the kitchen, poured the coffee, and inhaled the aroma of the pancakes. "That smells better than sex," she said as she leaned against the counter.

Kate lifted the spatula and sniffed the pancake before flipping it over. "What kind of sex are you having?"

Jamie smirked. "None of your business."

Kali stumbled into the kitchen. She maneuvered around Jamie, palmed the knob of the cabinet with outstretched hands and opened it without bending her fingers. She cupped a mug, then placed it on the counter.

"What's wrong with your fingers?" Jamie asked as she sipped her coffee.

"My fingers are so sore, they hurt when I bend them, so I have to keep them straight out."

"How'd that happen?" Kate asked.

"Victoria was hard to please this morning."

Kate held her arm straight out. "Whoa, whoa...I really do not want to hear about your sex life."

"I wasn't talking about sex. I was talking about her request for a morning foot massage. It killed my fingers." Kali showed her hands.

"Oh," Kate said.

"Yeah, oh. Geez, Kate, you need to get your brain out of the gutter. I swear, it's embarrassing to be around you at times." She turned to Jamie. "Would you mind filling my mug?"

Jamie poured some coffee and topped it off with a splash of almond milk. Kali palmed the sides of the mug. "Ouch, that's hot." She placed it back on the counter, leaned over it, and slurped.

"Speaking of Vic, where is she?" Jamie asked. Victoria had really pulled it all together yesterday. She was easy to work with, she could multitask like no one's business, and she coordinated the hell out of the wedding. Jamie said another silent prayer as she added those qualities to her never ending list of selfish reasons why she hoped Vic and Kali made it.

"She fell back to sleep after I gave her the foot massage. I quietly peeled out of bed and came down here."

Ruth materialized at the kitchen door. "Granola pancakes with blueberries?" She walked over to Jamie and kissed her. "Morning."

"How you feeling this morning, Ruth?" Kali chuckled as she gingerly wrapped her fingers around her warm mug.

"More normal. I just don't know what got into me last night."

Kali laughed. "I do."

"Pancakes are in the chafing dish. Grab a plate and help yourself," Kate instructed.

"Thanks." Ruth grabbed a plate out of the cabinet, stacked ten pancakes on top, and headed to the main room.

"Wish I could eat as much as I wanted and have it vaporize inside me," Kali said. "What a fantasy that would be."

"What did I just hear? You're fantasizing about my girlfriend?" Jamie grabbed a plate and headed to the chafing dish."

"Only her appetite, I swear."

"Well, guess I can't fault you there."

"Ever think about entering her in a hotdog eating contest?" Kali asked as she slowly started wiggling and massaging her fingers.

"What? Ew, no." Jamie forked a pancake on her plate, tore a piece off, and shoved it in her mouth. "Oh, that's good."

"I'm just saying, there might be a way to cash in on her special abilities."

"I'm going to pretend I didn't just hear that you want to pimp out my girlfriend as a food prostitute."

"If I had superpowers like Ruth, I'd figure out a way to exploit them."

"Can't hear you," Jamie mumbled.

Kate gently shoved a plate of pancakes into Kali's chest, then grabbed her own plate and followed them out of the kitchen. "You know, we do own a table," Kate said as everyone sat on the couch.

"Too formal." Jamie patted the space next to her.

"Fine," Kate muttered as she shuffled to the couch.

"Oh wow, I thought I smelled deliciousness." Victoria yawned as she made her way down the steps. She had bedhead, her T-shirt was on backward, and her boxers were hanging low on her hips.

"Coffee and pancakes are in the kitchen. I made extra, so take all you want."

"I don't see the pancakes." Victoria's voice floated out of the kitchen and into the main room with a hint of desperation and concern.

"They're in the chafing dish," Kate called through a mouthful of food. "I'm going to miss that dish when Annie comes by later this afternoon to pick everything up. I'm thinking I have to buy one."

Kali squeezed another layer of maple syrup over her pancakes. "I'll ask Annie if she has an older one she would be willing to sell."

"She's an excellent cook, Kali. I'm glad you two stayed on good terms." Jamie remembered the day Kali had announced she'd broken it off with Annie. The self-doubt in her eyes, the mopey depression that lasted for the remainder of that week, the *fuck it* shield that she put back on. Jamie had liked most of Kali's flings. They were good people. And every time she'd met one, she'd instantly felt sorry for them. It wasn't their fault; none of it was. They'd just happened to cross paths with Kali during her transition stage, which was now in its third year. *Wrong timing*, as Kali used to say. And maybe that really was true. As the cliché went, "You can't love someone if you don't love yourself." Jamie hoped that with Victoria, Kali would start loving herself again.

"She's a nice person and still sexy as hell." Kali shoved the last bite in her mouth and smiled as she chewed.

"Who's sexy as hell?" Victoria strolled out from the kitchen with a plate and a large mug that said, *Peace. Love. Coffee.*

"You are, babe. We were saying you're sexy as hell." Kali scooted over so Victoria could squeeze between her and Jamie. "Morning after look and all."

Kate winked. "Well, if that's the look after a night of wild sex, then sign me up."

"Again, Kate, you're embarrassing to be around. I was referring to the fact that my girlfriend can look sexy as hell the morning after a long and exhausting day's work. And for the record, we did not have wild sex last night. We were asleep by the time our heads hit the pillows."

Victoria playfully nudged her. "Don't go telling our secrets."

"There are no secrets around here," Kate and Jamie announced in unison.

"Here, here." Kali raised her mug in salute. "Oh hey, what time are the vendors coming?"

"I told them any time after one." Kate glanced at Jamie, who nodded.

"That'll work," Jamie agreed.

"Well, well, the star of the evening makes his appearance." Buddy jumped on the coffee table. Kate grabbed him and placed him and a small piece of pancake on the ground.

"Oh God." Jamie laughed. "You know that's going to get posted."

"Already has." Victoria turned her phone and showed everyone the picture of Buddy front and center cleaning himself on Leslie and Wendy's wedding page.

Kate took the phone. "Holy shit. It's already got four hundred and thirty-seven likes."

"What? Give me that." Kali grabbed the phone. "Damn. Maybe I should set up his own page?"

"Don't you dare." Jamie pointed her fork. "That's not the picture we want people to associate with our vineyard."

"Don't worry. Lesbians love their animals as much as their lovers, if not more." Victoria took her phone back.

"True," they all mumbled.

Wind chimes jingled from Jamie's phone. She looked at it, smiled, took a moment to type, then placed it back on the coffee table facedown. "It's nothing, babe, um, just a vendor." She lied again, and she guessed by her expression that Ruth knew it. She felt bad for keeping a secret. Ruth didn't deserve that, but Jamie needed to keep her in the dark for another hour or two. Then all would be revealed.

❖

That's what you keep telling me: it's just a vendor. Ruth felt like screaming as anxiety surged through her. This wasn't the first time Jamie had been texting or taking calls in a suspicious manner. For the past week, Jamie had either talked in a hushed voice while taking certain calls or turned her shoulder away while texting.

When Jamie had first started doing it, Ruth had shrugged it off and thought it was regarding the wedding, but lately, she had her doubts. In fact, she had almost convinced herself that Cheryl was back in the picture with yet another proposal.

A shiver of jealously hit her. Was Jamie second-guessing being with her? If she was, and Cheryl was back in the picture, how could Ruth possibly compete? With Cheryl, Jamie could enjoy all the things couples did: restaurants, shopping, trips. Ruth was stuck here with no money or means to give her the things others could.

What had she been thinking? She should have never approached Jamie. She should have left well enough alone. But she had become so lonely, so desperate to communicate with someone, so tired of waiting to transition. Being stuck on her tiny island of land as she watched people and time move around her was maddening. If Jamie and Cheryl really were getting back together, returning to that void of an existence would be worse than the death she'd suffered.

Ruth glanced at Jamie's cell phone and wished she understood more about the device so she could find the truth. But the technology baffled her. For a while, she'd thought people had been starting to go mad because they'd walked around the vineyard talking to themselves. After further observation, she realized a new communication device must have been invented. Jamie had tried to give her a crash course on how the phones worked, but she found it all too complicated. Besides, who was she going to call?

Jamie shoveled the last bite into her mouth, took a gulp of coffee, and gave a slight nod to Kate, who turned to Ruth and said, "Would you mind sticking around after breakfast and helping me with the dishes?"

Ruth looked to Jamie, then at Kate. She could feel the energy exchange between them, and it didn't feel right. *What was going on?* Ruth hated secrets. *Lillian held a secret, and look what happened.* "Um, of course I will."

"While you two are doing that, I'll go outside and do a tally of the items the vendors will be picking up this afternoon." Jamie gave her a peck on the cheek.

"I thought you and Kali did that last night?" Ruth could feel the rapid beating within her body, and she knew she was on the verge of pulsing and not for the right reasons.

"I know, sweetie. It's just that—"

"Some of it could be in the wrong pile since we did it when it was dark. In fact, I'll go with you." Kali jumped up and headed for the door.

"I'll help Ruth and Kate," Victoria called as she winked.

Ruth caught the gesture and stared her down. *You're in on this too?* Betrayal was something Ruth was all too familiar with. She felt sick to her stomach as she followed Kate and Victoria. She wanted to vanish and spy on Jamie, but a part of her said to trust in her lover. Then again, another part reminded her that trusting someone was what had gotten her killed.

As she followed Kate and Victoria into the kitchen, sadness settled in. Was she really destined to be alone through eternity?

❖

Kali turned to Jamie as they headed down the driveway. "Think she knows?"

"I'm sure she suspects something. She doesn't miss much."

"I know. And for the record, that's one of the reasons I don't think I could ever be with a ghost. They know too much."

Jamie laughed. "It's really not an issue when you have nothing to hide." She nudged Kali, knocking her off balance a bit.

"Still."

"So, Kal, what are you going to do with Vic?"

"Wow, what kind of kinky voyeur question is that?"

"What? No, I meant that she's wonderful, and I can already sense you pulling away. I starting notice it last week."

"Oh, that. Well then...yes and yes. I can't help it. Every time I think about how wonderful Vic is, I hear Cruella's voice telling me I'll never be good enough. You remember how she was in the end, all the things she said to me, and how she wiped me out."

"She was fucked up, Kali. Besides, why are you listening to her voice in your head instead of mine?"

"You know why."

"It's time to let it go. All of it."

"I can't." Kali shuffled ahead as she lowered her head. She'd met Cruella through an online dating app. She had hoped the profile picture of the woman flexing her muscles in a gym was an accurate representation because Kali had been instantly attracted to her. She'd classified Cruella as an athletic butch, a type she had never been with before, and fantasies of hard, intense sex had made her stomach react. It had taken two days before she'd gotten up the nerve to reach out to her, and Cruella's reply was immediate. Four days later, they were sitting opposite each other in a restaurant booth, sharing their life's stories over beer and pizza. Two hours later, Kali had gotten her first taste of what an arsenal of toys, in the hands of an experienced woman, could do to her body. By the end of that week, Kali had acquired a taste for pleasure that teetered on the verge of pain. The sex had been wild, erotic, exciting, and nothing like she had ever experienced, and it had been exactly what she'd needed.

The sex had been like a drug, and she'd gladly devoured an intoxicating dose night after night. Anything to take the edge off. To numb the emotional pain that had been ripping her heart in two for the past six months.

She'd known exactly what she was doing: trading the pain of losing her mom for the pain of pleasure. Same intense emotions just redirected. She'd wanted, no needed, someone to distract her. Someone to play a lead role in a life that was spinning out of control. This is only temporary, Kali had reassured herself. To take the edge off until I get over the hump and get my feet back on the ground.

But like most drugs, once invited in, they'd taken up residence and had quickly made themselves an unwelcome guest. Kali had been hooked before she'd seen the signs. Sex had become the fix, and Cruella had made sure Kali never broke free of its grasp.

Bit by bit, Cruella had begun to take over Kali's life. She'd dictated where they would go and who they would hang out with. She'd started planting seeds about how Kali's friends didn't have her best interests at heart, and that she would be better off without them.

With Kali's attention solely focused on her, Cruella had ramped up her masterful seduction. Thanks to the modest inheritance Kali had received after her mother's death, they'd had expensive vacations and shopping sprees. But the money hadn't lasted long, and after that was gone, so was Cruella. Apparently, Kali's "measly" salary as a graphic artist at the TV station hadn't covered the lifestyle Cruella had thought she deserved. Kali had known the end was near when the fighting had become more intense than the sex, and the drama had nothing to do with role-playing. With a bottomed-out bank account, mounting credit card debt, and more stress than she thought her body had been capable of coping with, Kali had finally reached out to the friends she had neglected for years. Some had rallied to her side; others had moved on.

"You're moving in with me, and I won't take no for an answer," Jamie had insisted one afternoon over lunch. "You can live for free or just pay for what you eat. Put your money toward paying down those cards, okay?"

"Thanks, Jamie. I uh, I don't know what to say." Kali had been touched Jamie was being so kind after all the times Kali had blown off their friendship because Cruella had whined about not liking her. *You are a better person than me.*

"Nothing to say. The spare bedroom is yours for as long as you need it. And a little friendly advice, you might want to take a break from women for a while and concentrate on healing."

Good advice, Kali had thought, but as she'd found out, hard to implement. The pull of addiction was strong, so Kali had compromised. She would continue to seek out women to satisfy her fix but would never commit to one. And in the meantime, she would try to get her shit together.

"Vic isn't Cruella. I get a really good vibe from her. She seems genuine," Jamie said.

"Ah, but that's how they all start out, then wham-o, they hit you with this totally psycho side when you're not looking."

Jamie laughed.

"I'm just saying."

"And I'm just saying, Vic seems like the real deal. Maybe it's time, Kali. Besides, she's your vibrator girl."

"I know, right. Kinda freaky, huh?" When Kali had created her dream girl, she'd imagined everything she wanted in a woman but thought was impossible to find. And if she were honest with herself, she'd hung that vision over the heads of her one-night stands as she'd told herself none of them had what she'd been looking for. Well, now one did, and it was scaring the shit out of her.

"Or...maybe it's magical."

"Says the woman who's getting it on with a ghost." Kali waved at the large flatbed truck slowly making its way up the road. They jogged to the end of the driveway and motioned for the driver to turn in. He rolled down his window.

Jamie reached up. "Hi, I'm Jamie, and this is Kali."

"Sam." He shook their hands. "Where's this going?"

"Southeast corner." Jamie pointed to the far side of the vineyard. "If you want, we can jump in and show you?"

"That'd be great." He cleared paperwork off his bench seat as Jamie and Kali climbed in. As they made their way to the southeast corner, Jamie guided him onto an area left undeveloped. "This is it."

He threw the truck in park and cut the engine. "Sounds good," he said as they all got out. He pulled a can of spray paint from his jacket and started shaking it. "Show me the exact spot you want it."

"Here." Jamie pointed to her feet and moved her hand back and forth in a straight line. Sam gave his spray can a final shake, then made a fluorescent pink X on the ground by her boots. "Yep, that'll work. Thanks, Sam. You need anything else from us?"

"Nope, paperwork says you prepaid, so give me about an hour, and she'll be all done."

"Sounds good. If you have any questions, just text me. I'll be at the house."

"Yep." He grunted as he heaved a large bag of mortar to the ground.

"Think she'll like it?" Kali asked as they headed back to the house. It was definitely an unusual gift to give someone, but from what Jamie had told her about Ruth's murder, it really was perfect.

"I sure hope so."

❖

"Everything okay?" Ruth asked with concern as Kali and Jamie entered the house.

Jamie gave her a kiss. "All good. Everything's separated and in place for when the vendors pick it up."

When Jamie's phone chimed, and she answered the texts without saying a word, Ruth had had enough. "Jamie, what is going on. You're scaring me."

"It's nothing, babe, just vendors with questions about picking up their stuff."

You're lying. Ruth saw it in her eyes. This wasn't about vendors or wedding stuff; this was about Cheryl. And an hour later, when Jamie excused herself to take a call in the kitchen, Ruth started pulsing. "Jamie, what is—"

"Ruth, sweetie, we have something to show you. Will you please wait in the house for fifteen minutes, then meet us at the southeast corner of the vineyard? You know the spot. I'll fill you in on the mysterious phone calls and text messages."

"Where I'm buried? Jamie, what's going—"

"Please, baby, everything will make sense in fifteen minutes. Promise me you'll wait here before meeting us. I'll set the kitchen timer because I know how you are about measuring time. Fifteen minutes, okay? Promise?"

Ruth nodded, but fear gripped her as she watched them leave. The next fifteen minutes felt like an eternity. She paced around the main room so much, Buddy gave up on his nap and left the room for a calmer space. Deep down, Ruth trusted Jamie, but that didn't mean her mind wasn't taking her down a dark road. She knew her instincts were dulled when her heart was in play. Her gut was telling her Cheryl was back in the picture. That Jamie was questioning being with her. And why not? Jamie needed someone that she could show off to other people, someone to experience all that life had to offer with.

The timer in the kitchen chimed, snapping Ruth back to the present. A blink later, and she was standing at her gravesite, face-to-face with Jamie. "I'm here. Now please tell me what is going on." Her world began to spin, and for the first time since her death, she felt crippling pain surge through her body. She looked in Jamie's eyes and searched for a hint of betrayal. "This is about Cheryl, isn't it?"

"Cheryl?"

"I know what's going on. I can feel—"

Jamie took a step to the right. A light gray, granite tombstone sat over the spot where Ruth had been buried so long ago. *RUTH* had been etched into the polished stone. And under her name, it read, *A soul never purer, a love never truer.*

"But how—" The crippling pain that had consumed her just moments ago dissipated as an odd feeling of lightheadedness came over her. She ran her fingers over the etched marble that spelled out her name. She thought it the most beautiful tombstone she had ever seen.

"We used some of the deposit money Legacy gave us for the wedding. Even Vic pitched in." Jamie motioned with her chin in Victoria's direction, and Ruth touched Vic's forearm. "You will never be forgotten, Ruth."

"I'm so sorry I doubted you."

Jamie leaned in and lovingly placed an arm around her shoulder. "This was never about Cheryl, Ruth, please don't ever think about her again. This is and always will be about you. I'm sorry if I made you think otherwise. I just wanted it to be a surprise."

"I, um, I don't know what to say." Ruth looked from her gravestone to the faces of those she now considered family. No one had ever been this kind to her.

"You don't have to say anything. I love you, baby. We all do."

"Thank you. Thank you so much," Ruth wiped tears from her eyes as they came together in a group hug. Maybe being stuck on this land truly was the best thing that had ever happened to her.

CHAPTER NINE

Kate picked a grape and squeezed three drops of juice onto the lens of the sloped end of the refractometer, a small cylinder-shaped device no longer than about six inches. Jamie stood next to her, biting her thumbnail and shifting her weight from foot to foot as she waited for the instrument to measure the sugar content of their fruit. The higher the sugar count, the better the grapes would be for fermenting.

"It looks like we're sitting at"—Kate held the refractometer against her right eye and faced the sun as though looking through a telescope—"twenty-three." She smiled.

"Woo-hoo." Jamie jumped up and fist bumped the air. And there it was, the day they had been waiting all year for. The harvest that would hopefully be enough to finally put the vineyard in the black and some money in their bank accounts.

"I'll call Mick and see if they can bring over the harvesters in the morning." Kate dug her phone out. "Mick, Kate here… We're sitting at twenty-three on the Brix test. How many harvesters can you spare…Really…Wow, that's perfect…Yep, see you at sunrise." She hung up. "He's sending over five."

Jamie nodded. "So what are we looking at?"

"One of Mick's machines can pick an acre an hour. With five?" She punched a series of numbers into her calculator app. "We're looking at a ten-hour shift to get the entire vineyard done. We have about two hundred tons of grapes this harvest, and at one ton equating to approximately two barrels of wine, minus the price Mick would knock off the top for the use of his harvesters…we should make a nice profit this year."

"Finally." Jamie exhaled as she began mentally spending the money. House repairs, a bigger barn for Ginger, marketing for their new private label, and a separate staging area for the many weddings they hoped would come.

"We should go tell Kali that between the harvest and the farmer's market, tomorrow's going to be a long day," Kate said.

Giddiness came over Jamie as they turned toward the house. She saw herself as a little girl running down this exact row so many years ago. Happy, carefree, and full of life. Back then, the vineyard had seemed so magical, so enchanting. Jamie smiled as she glanced at the ground, seeing the footprints of that little girl who ran in and out of these same vines playing a modified version of hide and seek. And as Jamie made new footprints over her old ones, marking her growth in time, she realized the magic of the vineyard still remained.

Kali was sitting on the porch bench, noticeably agitated. "Hey," Jamie said.

"Hey," Kali grunted in a drawn-out, dejected voice.

Jamie exchanged looks with Kate as they walked up the steps and sat on either side of her. "What's up?" Jamie placed a hand on her thigh.

"Vic's up."

Jamie let out a heavy sigh. "Did you guys break up?"

"No."

"Then what happened?"

Kali swiped on her cell phone, took a moment to maneuver, then handed it to Jamie. "Read what she just sent me."

Jamie glanced at the last conversation and read it out loud. "I'm sorry about what I said earlier. I think I'm just going to hang at my place for the weekend and catch up on a few things. Talk to you later." Jamie looked up. "What did she say earlier?"

"That she loved me."

Jamie leaned in and gave her a big hug. "Kali girl, that's awesome." Excitement surged through her. This was perfect. Kali and Victoria were in love, and now all her anxiety over Kali screwing up another potential relationship with a wonderful woman could be put to rest.

"Except I didn't return the words."

Kate leaned back. "Wait, you what? Why not?"

"I froze."

"As in, you left her hanging?" Jamie sighed. *Please don't do this again, Kali.*

Kate shook her head. "Damn, girl."

"Exactly. Now she doesn't want anything to do with me."

"That's not true. She's probably just feeling awkward," Jamie said. "And wait. I'm not understanding something here. You just told us the other night that you were in love with Vic. Why didn't you speak up?"

"I don't know. When she said the words, it sent butterflies around my stomach and all. I opened my mouth to tell her I love her too, I really did, but nothing came out. There was just this long, awkward silent pause of nothingness. Then she said she had to go…then this." Kali looked at Jamie. "I think she hates me."

Kate laughed. "Vic doesn't hate you. Obviously, she loves you. Call her back and tell her you do too."

"What? No, I can't do that."

"Why not?"

"Because now I feel like an asshole. I need to think about how I'm going to word this and then send her a text explaining everything."

"Or, circling back around to my original thought, you could call her and tell her you love her."

Kali stood and walked to the screen door. "I need to think about this, Kate. It's not that simple. It's complicated."

Kate looked to Jamie for guidance. "I don't get what's so complicated."

"Hey, Kali, just a heads up before you go in, the Brix is twenty-three, and Mick's sending over five harvesters at sunrise. That plus the farmer's market is going to make tomorrow an early morning."

"Twenty-three? Really? That's awesome! I need to tell Vic…oh wait." Her face turned somber. "Hmm, I need to think about this," she said as she looked at her phone and headed inside.

Kate turned to Jamie. "Please tell me this is a generation thing because holy hell, I'm still not getting it. Why doesn't she just call Vic?"

"It's complicated."

"So everyone keeps telling me."

"Just be grateful she's taking the time to think about it, instead of bolting. Trust me, that's a good sign for both of us. Now come on, let's start getting things ready for tomorrow. It's going to be a long one."

Kate stood on the front porch drinking coffee as Jamie and Kali came out to join her. The night sky gave way to the first glow of morning light. Five sets of ominous looking white lights pierced the thick morning fog as they slowly headed up the driveway. "Damn, that's impressive looking," Kali said as she snapped photos with her cell phone.

"Yeah, it never gets old," Kate mumbled as the anxiety she had been carrying all year dissipated. This harvest would be a good one. The climate hadn't thrown any curveballs their way this season, and the vines responded favorably. But Kate knew each year was becoming more and more of a crapshoot. Things were rapidly changing. Wildfires were becoming the norm, and the land she had come to know all these years as somewhat predictable was becoming very temperamental. And that was never a good sign, especially when the survival of the business depended on some level of predictability.

The harvesters were tall machines painted construction orange and split down the middle to allow the machine to perfectly straddle the grapevines and shake the fruit onto a conveyer belt that moved them to one of two collecting bins. When Kate and Nora had first noticed the new technology used on neighboring vineyards, they hadn't embraced the machines. They'd thought there would be more damage done to the fruit, but mostly, they'd felt bad that the hand pickers were losing income. But as technology had marched forward and more and more vineyards had started utilizing the machines, the labor force had dwindled. Eventually, Kate and Nora had given in and reluctantly joined the world of hi-tech harvesting.

"Good ol' Mick, he always comes through," Kate said as she sipped.

"I think it's time I disappear," Ruth announced and stepped into the house.

"I like it better when she just up and poofs away." Kali scoffed as she walked down the porch steps with Kate and Jamie. "Hell, I can disappear by walking into a house too. Where's the magic in that?"

The lead harvester broke away from the other four and made its way to the front of the house. The driver waved from a small cab about fifteen feet high and completely surrounded in glass, giving him a three-hundred-and-sixty-degree view. He climbed down the small metal ladder, took off his glove, and shook Kate's hand. "Kate."

"Bill, thanks for coming out so early." She held up a large carafe of coffee, several to-go cups, and nodded to the small basket of sweeteners and creams Jamie was holding. "For you and your crew." She'd known Bill for years. He had been her point person since she'd first made the deal with Chanadoah to harvest their crops. He was a sweet man, well respected in the community, and he and his team knew how to operate the machines with minimal crop loss.

"Appreciate it. How's it looking this season?"

"Good. We should have a nice harvest this time."

"Well, your place is sure looking good. I like what you've done to it."

"Bit by bit, you know how that goes."

"Tell me about it. Mary's still on me about wanting a kitchen upgrade. Unless she picks the winning lottery numbers, her little dream kitchen ain't happening anytime soon."

Kate nodded. "How's she doing these days?" The community of growers was small enough that the gossip mill was constantly churning. Kate had heard Mary wasn't feeling the best, and she had been meaning to bake a pie and bring it out.

"She's been nursing a bad back lately, so she's been taking it a little easy."

"Kate has a special batch of cookies that could remedy that," Kali threw out.

Kate smacked her on the shoulder as Bill chuckled. "I'll suggest it to her." He put his glove back on and climbed up his ladder. Kate handed him the carafe, cups, sweeteners, and creams. Bill placed them on his seat, then plopped next to them. "I'll have my guys start over there." He pointed to the far southwest corner. "We should have a full sweep of the vineyard by about"—he looked at his watch—"three or four this afternoon."

"Sounds good. I'll have food ready for you and your men whenever you need a break. Just shoot me a text, and we'll set it up."

"I'd never turn down one of your veggie and bean burritos."

"Well, then, you're in luck because that's exactly what's on the menu."

Bill smiled as he touched the computer screen mounted by his steering wheel. He waved, put the machine in motion, and headed toward the southwest corner. The four harvesters followed, split off, and within minutes, each straddled a row of vines. The harvest had begun.

"Thank God for machines. Could you just imagine if we had to pick the grapes ourselves?" Kali said. Ruth appeared by her side. "Oh, now you do the fancy ghost tricks?"

"I didn't feel like walking."

"Showoff."

"Kali, I need you to grab shears and a bucket and head over to the garden. We need to take a haul of grapes to the market this morning." Kate and Nora had designated a quarter of an acre by Ginger's barn for growing table grapes for their own consumption and to take to the local farmers market. Their close friends, Jan and Sheri, rented a space there, and Kate and Nora always donated several buckets of produce. Their fresh grapes always sold out. The money went to the animal shelter

Jan and Sheri volunteered for. Through the years, they had been able to donate thousands of dollars from their grapes, and because of that, Kate took their garden harvest as serious as their vineyard. Giving back to the community was what Nora had taken joy in. A bittersweet feeling surrounded Kate as she headed toward the garden. *Your grapes are looking beautiful, babe. They'll sell well at the market today. Good job.*

"Okay, I'll get right on it as soon as I finish another cup. That last one hasn't successfully coursed through my veins and taken over my brain yet."

"Ruth, would you mind going inside and filling a to-go mug for Kali? The market opens at eight. We need to get the grapes dropped off no later than seven thirty, so we need to get moving."

"You know, Kate, this whole dominatrix thing you've got going on right now is really turning me on," Kali teased as she picked up a bucket and shears and huffed her way to the garden.

"What's a dominatrix?" Ruth asked Jamie, who whispered the answer in her ear, causing Ruth to pulse.

"Happy now, Kali? You just embarrassed a ghost."

"Welcome to the house of heathens." Kali laughed as she spread her arms and spun around.

Kate chuckled. What would life be without Jamie and Kali? They always had a way of filling the black hole of loneliness that crippled her from time to time. Without them, she couldn't imagine what her book of life would look like. One thing was for sure, it would be a sad and pathetic one.

❖

Kali loaded the back of Kate's F-150 blue pickup with a dozen five-gallon buckets of grapes. Kate and Jamie secured the buckets with rope as Ruth handed Kali a travel mug filled to the brim. "Have you had new shocks put on this 1995 thing recently?" Kali asked Kate as she took the mug and nodded a thank you to Ruth.

"Nope," Kate replied as Kali opened the door and hopped in.

"Shit, Kate, last time I drove the truck, my boobs bounced so much they hurt for days."

"You wearing one of your fancy sports bras this morning?"

"Yeah."

"Well, then, don't worry about it. You'll be just fine. Now, go on, get outta here and tell Jan and Sheri we say hello. Come on." Kate motioned to Jamie. "We need to start making lunch for Bill's crew."

Kali closed her door and took a sip of coffee. "Damn, Ruth, that tastes perfect. Thanks."

"You're welcome."

Kali threw the truck in drive and headed away. As she took a right onto the road, she put her Bluetooth earbuds in and played a song from her playlist. She bobbed her head, tapped on the steering wheel, and loudly sang along. She glanced at the empty space beside her, and her thoughts drifted to Victoria.

Kali hadn't sent the text explaining herself. Something seemed off as she read it, deleted it, started over, deleted that one, started over...and repeat, repeat, repeat. She typed and retyped a long confession about how much she missed Victoria and how wonderful their relationship was. How for the first time in a long time, she'd felt whole with someone. She wanted Vic to know that she was not a fling like her other distractions. Okay, maybe at first she was, but Kali soon realized that Vic was different. Or maybe, just maybe, she was the one who was different. She was no longer craving the addiction of distraction sex. Being with Vic actually made her want to stay in the present and feel real feelings again.

"Shame," Kali whispered the word that put the train wreck of her life in motion. "Shame," she said again and tasted the way the word felt on her lips. The word she'd given so much power to and the emotion behind it that she ran from.

Jamie used to tell her to let it go, to take herself off the hook, but Kali was her own worst critic. She allowed shame to take up residence and wreak havoc in her mind, all logic be damned. It was so much easier to hang on to something and replay it over and over in her head, as though changing the ending in her mind would somehow change the ending in time. Wishful thinking.

Her mom had to die when she did, no matter what. The doctors had reassured Kali that the aneurysm was most likely a result of her mom's battle with type one diabetes and all the health complications that came with it. But Kali had convinced herself that the fight she'd had with Mom that morning over politics had been the contributing factor.

She'd hung her head in guilt and shame over the last words she'd spoken and had used that as a battle cry to drown herself in sex-medicated destructive behavior. But Jamie was right; maybe it was time she stopped the shame-train. That didn't mean that she wasn't still a bit fucked up. It just meant that maybe the beginning of a long road of healing could finally begin.

Five songs later, as Kali pulled into the market, she made a promise to herself to send Victoria the last text still sitting in her phone, and hopefully by tonight, they would be in each other's arms, engaged in make-up sex. Damn it, Kali chided herself, stop with the sex. *Conversation...she meant she hoped they would be in each other's arms engaged in make-up* conversation. *Geez.*

She scanned the small market for Jan and Sheri's tent as she inched up the area designated for vendors. It only took a few seconds to spot the produce truck with their logo, Gracie's Organic Farm, painted on the side. Gracie, their friendly ten-year-old Husky mix from the Humane Society, was framed inside the "O" of organic.

Kali parked next to their truck and jumped out. "Hey, Jan. Hey, Sheri," she called as they turned and waved. "I have a dozen five-gallon buckets full of super sweet grapes." She hoisted one of the buckets out and brought it over. "Where do you want me to...what the hell happened to you?"

Jan had her right foot in a blue medical boot. "We were rearranging the furniture, and the bookcase fell on my big toe. Crushed the nail, blood everywhere, and it hurt like hell."

"Yeah, I almost fainted when I saw it." Sheri grabbed Kali's bucket and gently shook the contents into a bin sandwiched between heads of lettuce and clusters of beets.

"Damn, girl." Kali bent to get a full look at the damage.

"Yep, there goes hiking and biking for a while."

"Yeah, I bet." Kali took the empty bucket and headed back to her truck to get more. "Why don't I stick around and help you guys out this morning? Looks like she's struggling a bit." Kali enjoyed Jan and Sheri. They were school teachers by day and organic farmers and shelter volunteers every other time. They worked hard but didn't have a lot to show for it. If the vineyard's wedding business picked up, she would hook them up with Annie as the organic produce supplier for the vineyard's recommended caterer. It would be a win-win all the way around.

"Seriously? Do you have time?" Sheri sounded relieved as she hustled to unload more produce.

"Yeah, no worries. Just let me refill my coffee mug from Kathy's tent. You guys want anything?"

"A muffin and one of her signature warm pretzels. Grab a twenty out of my purse. It's on the front seat of our truck."

"Nah, I got it." Kali grabbed the to-go mug out of Kate's truck, stuffed a handful of grapes in her arms, and walked two tents over. "Trade ya." She set a cluster of grapes and her mug on Kathy's table and leaned in to give her a big hug. Kali loved this community and everyone in it. They were good people, and they would always pitch in to help a neighbor in need. Being a local in this town meant you were family.

"Kali! You know your bribery is no good here, but I graciously accept." She reached for Kali's mug and refilled it. "You dropping a load off with Jan and Sheri?"

"Yep, and I'm sticking around. A bookcase fell on Jan's big toe and smashed it. She's not getting around too well in that boot thing."

"Ouch, that had to hurt. How's the vineyard doing?"

"Mick's guys are there now harvesting. I think this year we should see some profit."

"That's awesome. Can I get you anything else?"

"Yeah, a muffin for Jan and one of your pretzels for Sheri." She reached in her pocket and pulled out a twenty.

"Nope, it's on me. They gave me a huge bag of produce last week that was absolutely delicious."

Kali smiled. Yep, it was just like Jan and Sheri to do that. She jumped ahead in her thoughts. If her and Vic really did make it, she'd ask Vic to live at the vineyard. The city she lived in an hour and a half away had no sense of community. Everyone kept to themselves. Hell, Vic said she didn't even know her neighbors.

"Thanks, Kath, I'll let them know."

"I threw in an extra pretzel for you."

"Coffee and a warm pretzel? You know you're talking dirty to me, girlfriend."

Kathy laughed and shooed Kali along. "Give my love to Jamie and Kate, and come back over for more refills."

"Thanks. Tell Sandy I said hi." Kali returned to Jan and Sheri's tent and handed over the bag of deliciousness.

"Damn, that smells good," Sheri said as she grabbed the muffin and a pretzel. "Is the second pretzel yours?"

"Yep, Kathy threw it in after I bribed her. Oh, she also said she owed you guys for the bag of produce, so these are on her."

"That was nice of her," Jan said as they paused to enjoy their treats before they turned cold. "We should probably finish setting up."

"Yep, on it." Kali shoved the remaining bit of pretzel in her mouth, brushed the salt off her fingers, and helped her prepare for the rush of locals waiting for the market to open.

The event was free every Saturday morning from eight until eleven, with the most crowded time between eight and nine. If the surge of locals was any indication, today was going to be a profitable day. The produce was moving fast, and Kali was so busy restocking, she didn't have time to float back to her normal mental rants or worry about her current status with Victoria.

"We need more grapes," Sheri called as she rang up customers.

"On it." Kali hurried to her truck, grabbed the remaining two buckets, and rushed back. She gently dumped them in their designated area, grabbed a container of potatoes under the table, and began restocking the bin when she caught a whiff of the perfect mix of patchouli and sandalwood. She stopped as a shiver raced down her body causing her nipples to stand at attention.

"Hi," Victoria whispered from directly behind her.

Without even thinking, Kali grabbed her, pulled her into a tight hug, and kissed her. A man cleared his throat as he tried to reach around them.

"Oh, sorry." Kali linked fingers with Victoria and shuffled her to her truck. "I missed you so much. I'm such an idiot. I just, it's just, when you told me you loved me, I kinda, um…"

"Froze."

"Exactly. Not because I don't love you. I do love you. It's just sometimes, I get in my own way. In fact, I've kinda been getting in my own way for the past several years." She gently brushed a strand of hair out of Victoria's eyes and gave her a passionate kiss.

❖

When Victoria pulled away, she cupped Kali's face with her hands and looked her in the eyes. She had been on edge since their conversation and had prepared herself for the worst. Hearing Kali say, "I love you," made her heart sing. She'd known Kali would disconnect after they had passionate and intense sex or when Vic wanted to dive deeper into what had happened with Kali's mom.

And she'd heard the smirk in Paige's voice every week at work when she'd *just happened* to check in and ask her how things were going with Kali by saying, "Wow, you're still together."

Victoria wasn't stupid. She knew the risk she was taking with her heart. But damnit, she was in love, and she would rather be vulnerable and risk getting shot down, then continue in a relationship where she was half-present because she was fearful that expressing her emotions would upset her lover. "Babe, you're my everything. You will always be my everything."

"But…"

"But nothing. I love you."

"I love you too, Vic, I really do."

"Hey, Kali, can you grab more lettuce?" Sheri called.

"Yep, be right there. I gotta go. Why don't you come over to the house for dinner tonight and um, stay?"

"I'd like that very much."

Kali kissed her again, "See you tonight." She stepped over to Jan and Sheri's truck. "Oh, and Vic?"

"Yeah?"

"Maybe we can spend some time talking. It's time I shared a few more things with you."

"I'd like that," Vic smiled as she walked away and merged with the sea of shoppers. *God I'm into that woman.*

CHAPTER TEN

Ruth was sitting with Ginger in the barn, keeping her company and telling her about the day's events, when Ginger started whinnying, throwing her head, and pacing around her stall. "What is it, girl?" Ruth reached out to settle her, but Ginger remained in an agitated state.

Ruth's senses came on high alert. She's learned a long time ago to pay attention to the behavior of animals; they had a lot to say if she listened. Whatever Ginger was trying to tell her was sending a chill up Ruth's spine. Something was close, and whatever that something was, it was terrifying.

Ruth backed away from the stall and ran outside. "Oh my God." She gasped as fear surged through her. "No, no, no, not that." Fire was the one thing she feared the most. She'd once sat invisible at the firepit with Nora and Kate when a rather large spark flew out and landed on her lap. Crippling pain hit her as the ember seared through her body. It had taken days before she was able to heal, and during that time, the pain remained at an intense level. If her body reacted like that from just a spark, what was coming down the hill would surely destroy her.

Of all things, why this and why now? Ruth ran into the house and screamed, Fire!" She materialized up the stairs, continuing to yell as she banged on the bedroom doors. "Everyone, get up now!"

❖

"Jamie pulled a T-shirt over her head as she walked into the hallway. "What is it, babe, what's going on?" The look in Ruth's eyes sent a chill up her. "Ruth, what is it, what happened?"

Kali stumbled out of her bedroom, rubbing her eyes. "Yeah, what's going on?"

"The hills are on fire, and the wind is blowing this way."

"What?" Jamie ran down the stairs and onto the front porch. Kali and Victoria were right on her heels. Kate peeled herself off the couch and hurried behind them.

"Holy shit," Jamie mumbled as she stood frozen, watching the red flames dance across the hills in the distance, a deep red glow illuminating the sky. A strong acidic smell mixed with the distinct odor of burning wood filled the air. It had been several months since their harvest, and Northern California had been having a string of wildfires lately, but none of them had been close enough to worry about. On the news, all the homes had been burned to the ground, and tearstained survivors talked about losing everything they had. But that was in other parts of the state, not here. Sure, everyone knew the threat was real, but Jamie had never wanted to believe it would happen to them.

An emergency alert blared from Kate's phone, prompting everyone to stumble back into the house. "They've already started evacuating Clarksdale." Kate held her phone out so everyone could see.

Victoria grabbed the remote off the coffee table and frantically flipped between two of the local early morning news programs. "…it's spreading fast to the east. As of now, we can confirm over five thousand acres and several houses have already been lost, as forced evacuations are beginning…"

"We have to get Ginger out of here," Kate said. "Jamie, get the trailer hitched up, and someone find Buddy."

Jamie grabbed keys by the front door and headed for Kate's pickup. With shaky hands, she tried to push the key in the ignition but misjudged, and the keys dropped to the floor by her feet. "Shit." She fumbled around to find them. Finally, her fingers wrapped around the keyring, and with a second attempt, she was able to jam the key into the ignition and turn the engine. She threw the truck in reverse and backed to a rusty horse trailer. She rolled down the window and yelled, "A little help here!"

Kali and Kate flew out of the house. "You guide her in while I get Ginger," Kate said as she ran into the barn.

"Okay Jamie, keep coming back." Kali waved. "A little more…stop."

Jamie flew out of the truck, grabbed the crank handle on the trailer, and lowered it onto the ball of the truck's hitch. "Trailer's ready, Kate."

❖

"Easy there, girl. Come on now, sweetie, it's okay, we're going to get you out of here." Ginger was whinnying loudly and throwing her head. "Easy, girl, easy." Kate placed her hand on Ginger's face by her muzzle. "That a girl, easy…easy." She slowly put the halter over Ginger's nose, but Ginger threw her head, and the halter went flying. "Shit!" Kate retrieved it and tried again. "Come on, girl, let's get you out of here." *Come on, sweetie, work with me. We've got to get out of here. I can't lose you, not now. Not after losing Nora.*

"Kate, we need to get going," Kali yelled.

Kate maintained eye contact with Ginger as she slowly approached. Ginger was more than just a horse. She was Kate's go-to when the pain from Nora's death felt like it was suffocating her. She was Kate's morning therapy session and her evening wind down. Kate loved her with all her heart, and she would do everything in her power to protect her.

She took a moment to rub Ginger's face as she gently slipped the halter over her head. She slid the stall door open and held tight to the lead rope. Ginger spooked as Kate walked her out of the barn. Kate pressed a hand into her nose, tucking her head, which gave Kate more control. "It's okay, baby, you're okay. I promise, I'm going to get you out of here."

"Finally," Jamie said.

Kate walked Ginger up the ramp and into the trailer. She tied her off, closed the doors, and hopped in the truck.

Victoria ran out of the house, leaning to the right under the weight of a navy-blue cat crate. "All the roads west and south are blocked. You'll have to go north." She heaved the crate through the open window.

Kate gently placed a yowling Buddy on the seat beside her. "Shit, the northern roads aren't great hauling roads on a good day, much less running from a fire." And they'd be slow going. She could only do about thirty-five miles per hour. If the wind picked up or shifted in anyway, she could easily be trapped.

Jamie waved her forward. "Go, get out of here! Text when you're safe and let us know where you are."

Kate threw the truck in drive, "I'll head to Carmen's place." *Nora baby, watch over us and pull some strings if you can.*

❖

Jamie headed for the house. As Kate pulled down the driveway, sirens began to wail in the distance. "Grab the hoses and wet down the house, and let's turn the irrigation on full. Maybe if we flood the rows, it'll help."

They scattered, Jamie and Kali headed to the side of the house to open the irrigation controls. Ruth and Victoria grabbed hoses and started spraying the porch.

"Keep an eye on that fire, Kali. If you think it's accelerating or the wind changes, we need to get out of here," Jamie said as they opened one irrigation line after the other.

After about thirty minutes, a patrol car sped up their driveway, sirens flashing. It skidded to a stop, and an officer ran toward them. "You need to evacuate."

"How bad is it?" Jamie glanced at the hills.

"Picking up speed. The wind is shifting. Just got word it's heading for Chanadoah's property."

The words were like a punch to Jamie's gut. "Are the northern roads still possible?"

"Barely."

Jamie said a silent prayer that Kate, Ginger, and Buddy had made it through the pass and were safely on their way to Carmen's small ranch on the outskirts of the city. The fact that she hadn't received a text was chewing at her gut.

"Now," the officer said before he returned to his car and sped off.

"Let's take my car," Victoria called. She hopped in her SUV.

Kali emerged from the house. "I've got our purses. Come on, you guys, let's get out of here."

Jamie turned to Ruth, whose body began to shake. Ruth had told her over and over that she couldn't leave the land, but there was no way Jamie was leaving without her.

"Baby, we need to get out of here," Jamie said.

"I can't. Don't you think I've tried? I've spent so many years of my life trying to leave this land, and I can't."

"But, baby—"

Ruth ran past Jamie to the edge of the property, stopped, and turned. She took several steps backward until some invisible boundary began chewing her up, and the disintegrated particles of her body floated away in the air.

"Stop," Jamie yelled in fear as she ran in Ruth's direction. *What the hell?*

Ruth fell forward, the particles reforming her body.

Jamie threw her arms around her, tears blurring her vision. "Baby, I won't leave you."

"You have to," Ruth cried. "You have to leave now. Get Kali and Victoria far away from here."

Kali slapped the roof of the car as she yelled, "Let's go."

"I'm not leaving you," Jamie cupped Ruth's face as she touched their foreheads together. "You are my everything. I'll stay with you."

"Guys, we need to go, now," Kali screamed.

"No," Jamie shouted back. "I can't leave Ruth!"

Ruth grabbed Jamie's hand and ran to the car. Jamie stumbled behind.

"Kali, get her out of here," Ruth pleaded.

"Both of you, get in the car." The level of fear in Kali's shaky voice was undeniable.

"She can't leave the vineyard." Jamie choked on the words. Her heart felt like it was being ripped open.

Kali looked at Ruth. "At all?"

"I'll be fine, I'm already dead. But you need to get out of here before it's too late."

Kali finally nodded and grabbed Jamie's forearm. "Jamie, we have to go."

Jamie pulled away. "You go. I'm staying."

"You are not."

"I am staying with Ruth."

"Ruth will be fine."

"You don't know that!"

"I know that if we don't leave right now, that fire's going to kill us all. Now come on." Kali grabbed Jamie and pulled her toward the car.

The world began to spin around Jamie as Kali dragged her closer to the car and farther from Ruth. *This can't be happening. This isn't real. I need Ruth right now. I need her to tell me everything will be okay.* Jamie beat at Kali's arm. She needed to break free. She needed to be with her love.

As Jamie ran back to Ruth's arms, a chilling sensation tickled up Ruth's body as a layer of smoke and heat settled upon them. Ruth slowly glanced over her shoulder as the fire crested the hill. Fear welled inside her as she turned back to Jamie and yelled, "Run!"

And there it was, the word spoken to her so long ago. The word Lillian had screamed with such emotion and fear. And now she was doing the same to Jamie. Ruth hadn't made it to the woods that night, but right now, Jamie had a chance.

"Run, Jamie, far away from here." Ruth placed a hand on Jamie's face and pulled her into a long kiss. If the fire reached Ruth, it would destroy her. She was not going to make it out of this. But Jamie had a shot if she left now. Ruth pulled out of the kiss, locked eyes with the only person who had ever made her feel loved, and she knew what she needed to do.

Victoria honked the horn. Tears streamed down Ruth's cheeks. She took three steps back, said, "Be safe my love," and disappeared.

❖

"No. No, Ruth *no!*" Jamie's scream filled the air.

Kali locked her arms around Jamie's waist and forced her to the car. Jamie twisted to free herself, but Kali tightened her hold. "Open the back door," Kali called. Victoria flung the back door open. Kali wrestled Jamie into the car and slammed the door. She jumped into the passenger seat. "Lock her in."

Vic hit the child safety button. "Where's Ruth?"

"She'll be fine." Kali tried to sound convincing, even though deep down, she wasn't sure if they would ever see Ruth again.

Victoria threw the SUV into gear and raced down the driveway. As she made a hard left onto the paved road, her tires skidded, causing the SUV to rock from side to side. "Northern or eastern roads?"

"We heading to your place?"

"Yep."

Kali took a moment to swipe through her phone. "Right… go right!" Vic made a hard right, slowing down just enough to keep all four wheels on the road. "Looks like we should be good all the way to the freeway. I'm going to call Kate."

Straight to voice mail: *I'm out doing something fun, so leave a message…beep.*

"Hey, Kate, we're headed for Victoria's apartment. Call us and let us know you're okay." She didn't like that Kate didn't pick up, and worst-case scenarios began pounding in her head.

Vic motioned to the back seat. "How's she doing?"

Jamie was curled up in a ball with her hands wrapped around her head. Kali turned back to Victoria and shook her head with concern.

"Holy shit!" Victoria jerked the wheel. The SUV swerved as a fireball of debris rolled across the road.

Jamie popped her head up, "what was that?"

"Better buckle up, Jamie, things could get rough." A tightness gripped Kali's chest, as she let out a breath. Once they hit the open freeway, according to her fire app, it should have been safe sailing all the way to Victoria's apartment. But the area between where they were and the freeway was completely red on her screen. Fortunately, there were no other cars on the road, so as Vic sped through the hills, she could take each turn fast and wide.

"Freeway's about a mile out." Kali sighed in relief but could still feel the tightness in her chest. Even though the fire was burning dangerously close on both sides of the hills, the road was mostly unaffected.

Vic nodded.

The roads that wound through the area were dark and tricky to maneuver on a clear night, much less one that had hazy smoke lingering like a semi-dense fog at the base of the hills. Kali started bouncing her leg, to help release some of the pent of energy. She knew a sharp turn was ahead, one Vic needed to take with caution. After that, it would be a straight sprint to the freeway. She rubbed the sweat off her hands and onto her jeans. She needed to stay calm for Vic's sake, but the stress she was feeling was surging through her veins and giving her a bad case of the jitters.

"Holy shit." An uneasy feeling chilled Kali as they began rounding the hairpin curve. "Where is all this smoke coming from?"

A dark mass of thick smoke engulfed their car, bringing the visibility down to almost zero. Victoria slowed. They crept through the last part of the curve. "Damn." Vic exhaled. "I can hardly see around this...oh my God!"

On the other side of the turn, fire devoured both sides of the road. Flames shot fifteen feet in the air, and sparks began dancing around the car like a swarm of fireflies.

"Turn around Vic, holy hell, turn around," Jamie yelled.

"Vic, turn around," Kali echoed. She began breathing faster as her muscles tensed. She felt so much adrenaline shoot through her, she had to suppress the urge to bolt out of the car and run. *We're going to be trapped.*

Vic slammed on the brakes and threw the car in reverse as a thunderous crash rang out behind them. "Shit," Vic whispered. A tree lay across the road, consumed in flames and blocking their escape.

They were trapped with no way out. Vic closed her fingers around the steering wheel, took a deep breath, and threw the car in drive. "Hold on." She punched the accelerator, and the SUV leaped forward.

Kali placed one hand on the dashboard and gripped the roof handle. Burning debris exploded on the car as they raced forward. Kali began hyperventilating, and her skin crawled with the sensation of being poked by hundreds of pins and needles.

"Come on, girl. Come on, girl," Victoria said as she pressed the accelerator to the floor. Pieces of burning wood rained down on them, hitting the roof with such force, it sounded like someone was using a baseball bat.

"Shit." Kali rolled down her window, leaned to her left, and kicked at a piece of burning wood that had lodged between the door and side view mirror. Thick smoke slithered inside the car, and everyone began coughing.

"Roll…the window…up," Jamie choked as she rubbed her face on her sleeve.

Kali gave a final kick to the wood, and it dislodged, bursting into tiny burning fragments on the pavement. She hit the button, and the window creaked up. The smell of burned leather caught her attention, and she noticed smoke coming from her singed boots. "Shit." She slapped at the leather. "Damn, that was close."

"Yeah," Vic said as she hunched forward. She wiped her eyes on her sleeve again as she squinted at the road. The headlights were all but useless as the light from the halogen beams scattered in the smoke. "I can barely see anything out—"

Bang. Victoria lurched against the seat as the windshield cracked.

Jamie screamed.

"What the fuck was that?" Victoria leaned to her left as she tried to see out of a small section of glass that didn't resemble a spiderweb.

"I think it was a tree branch," Kali yelled over the maddening sound of debris pelting the car. She looked out the rear window and noticed splintered wood bouncing on the pavement behind them.

"Come on, baby," Vic said. "Almost there...almost..."

Kali rocked back and forth as if doing so would help gain speed. "Vic." She fearfully pointed to the left side of the road where a tree was completely engulfed in flames and beginning to lean toward them.

"I see it."

Kali tightened her muscles and prepared for impact. The tree swayed like a dead giant about to fall. "Vic!"

"I know!"

"It's going to hit us, Vic, stop the car. Stop the car."

"I've got it, I've got it."

"No, you don't, stop the car."

Kali dug her fingers into the dashboard as the car sped forward. "Please, please, please," she whispered in prayer as she closed her eyes. Her throat began to burn with the mixture of stomach acid and smoke. "This is insane." She turned to stare at Victoria as she swallowed back the threat of last night's dinner making a reappearance.

"Hold on," Victoria mumbled.

The orange glow from the fire was almost blinding as the SUV approached. Sparks popped all around them, and the tree took on an ominous look as flames shot out from the core. "We're not going to make it." Saliva was building in Kali's mouth, and her head pounded as fast and hard as her heartbeat. *We're going to die. Oh my God, we're going to die.*

"We're going to make it."

Boom! Kali closed her eyes as the SUV collided with parts of the tree. Her body jerked to the side, the seat belt digging into her as the car lurched to the right. Sweat beaded down her face as the sauna-like heat building in the car became suffocating. Another loud hit to the car popped her eyes open.

"We're on fire! Holy shit, we're on fire," Jamie yelled.

The entire windshield was covered in flaming debris. "Vic, stop the car, it's going to explode," Kali pleaded.

"Just a little farther..." She leaned forward as she mumbled, "Almost...almost."

"Vic," Kali pleaded, then added, "pull over." The sparks began to clear, and Vic brought the car to a screeching halt. Kali jumped out, bent over, and heaved her guts on the side of the road.

"Kali." Jamie jumped out and placed a hand on Kali's back. "You okay?" She coughed.

Victoria ran over and choked, "Everyone okay?"

Kali nodded as she wiped the back of her hand across her mouth. "How's the...car?" She spit in an attempt to clear the vile taste from her mouth as she stood up on shaky legs.

"I think it's okay, but we really need to go," Vic said as she ran back to the driver's side.

Kali turned and squinted at the car. Her eyes were watering so much, her vision was blurred. Smoke from sections of the SUV mixed with the dense air, but she couldn't see any flames.

"Get in the car, now," Vic yelled as she leaned over the seat.

Kali and Jamie hopped back in, and Vic threw it in drive. Kali wiped her eyes on her shirt, then took a moment to glance out the rear window. The fire was behind them. They'd made it. Kali whispered, "You did good, babe."

Vic turned to Kali and nodded

"You were amazing."

"Yeah." Victoria began to shake.

Kali placed a reassuring hand on her thigh and squeezed. "You did good," she repeated.

❖

Vic nodded as she took a deep breath and coughed it out. Adrenaline was still surging through her body, and her muscles were so tense, they were starting to ache. What the hell did she just do? Driving through a burning tree, what was that? She could have gotten everyone killed. She was in such a trance-like state, she barely remembered doing it. She wiggled her fingers on the steering wheel and tilted her head from shoulder to shoulder to try to loosen the tension. *But we made it.* Kali's words raced around her head. *We made it.*

Moments later, she turned onto the freeway heading north, and Kali rolled her window down, letting the fresh air purge the last remnants of smoke from the car. They continued in silence, each lost in their own thoughts. What words could possibly define what they just went through? Later, Vic was certain, they would each tell an animated version of the harrowing event to friends and family.

She leaned her head out her window as the warm air blew over her. The air still smelled of smoke, but the density had thinned.

Twenty minutes later, she eased the car into her designated parking space in the quaint apartment complex that housed fifty units. She threw the car in park and let out a deep breath. It was over; they were safe. Kali wrapped her hand around her neck and pulled her to her lips. The adrenaline that was still surging through her body played out in the hard and passionate kiss.

When they finally broke, Vic whispered, "Let's get settled in."

Kali nodded as she turned to Jamie. "Let's go."

Jamie blinked and unbuckled her belt. She looked around and in a far-off voice asked, "Where are we?"

"We're at my apartment."

Jamie nodded.

Victoria peeled herself from the car and stood in stunned disbelief as she looked at her SUV from under the parking structure's fluorescent lights. The silver paint had all but burned off, deep scratches down the side looked like a rabid werewolf had attacked, the entire car was pockmarked as if they'd drove through an unimaginable hail storm, and the windshield might as well have done a faceplant into a brick wall. They were damn lucky to be alive.

Kali flung her backpack and Jamie's purse on her shoulder. "Come on, let's go get cleaned up."

❖

Jamie scooted out of the car. She had a headache from the combination of crying, screaming, and smoke inhalation. The entire drive on the freeway, she'd thought of nothing but Ruth, and right now, she felt like her entire lifeforce had been sucked out of her body. She shuffled, one foot in front of the other, as she followed and gave no thought to the direction as they walked up a flight of stairs. Moments later, she flopped on Vic's couch in the small, sparsely furnished, one-bedroom apartment. She looked around the room yet saw nothing. She was stuck in a dream-like state, waiting to wake up.

Kali sat down next to her and in a faraway voice, said, "I'm going to send Kate a text letting her know we are safe."

Jamie nodded, at least she thought she did, but she wasn't really sure. Reality still played out in a foggy way in front of her. Vic flipped on the TV. The unfamiliar voices of the reporters rattled off sections of the area that were in the fire zone. According to the news, their vineyard was probably engulfed in fire. Jamie leaned into Kali and sobbed.

An acoustic guitar strummed from Kali's phone. "It's Kate," she said as she swiped the screen and hit the speaker. "How are you? How's Ginger and Buddy?"

"We...it...out...over at..."

"Kate, you're breaking up really bad. Can you repeat that?"

"The...road...trailer was almost...but we're okay."

The line went dead, and Kali's multiple attempts to call back failed.

"She said she was okay, so until we hear back from her, let's go with that," Kali said as she tossed the phone on the coffee table. "For now, who wants a shower?"

Jamie felt a hand slip under her arm and lift her up. "Come on, let's get you in first." She stumbled alongside Kali into the bathroom. She blinked and jerked her head when Kali hit a switch, and the bright light assaulted her.

"Hands up," Kali said in a soft voice.

Jamie automatically did as she was told until she felt the coolness of the room against her naked body. She shivered but didn't make a move to do anything about it. Eventually, the steam from the running water slowly warmed her skin.

"Let's get you in." She guided Jamie into the shower.

As soon as Jamie placed her head under the water, it broke her dream-like state. A vision of Ruth smiling danced before her. "Ruth," Jamie whispered, and her heart sank. She had no idea what they would return to once they were cleared to go home, but she feared Ruth would not be there. She placed her head in her hands, slowly sank to the floor of the shower, and curled up in a ball. As the water sprayed over her body, she let it carry her tears down the drain.

After three days, the authorities announced the fire was eighty percent contained, and by the fifth day, the local sheriff's department declared that the blaze was completely out. The area still needed to be checked for downed power lines, but there was a hotline with up-to-date information on when residents could return. The sheriff's department also warned that everyone should be aware that the burned debris could be a toxic hazard and that they should be cautious as they began returning to their land.

Jamie called the hotline. A robotic voice rattled off several all-clear zones, then proceeded to say that if their property was not mentioned, they were not allowed to return. Unfortunately, the vineyard was not in the zone, so they had no choice but to wait. Jamie tossed her phone on the coffee table and placed her head in her hands. The agony of waiting was excruciating. She was exhausted but couldn't sleep. She went for walks around the complex when the silence of the night was more than she could handle. And when Victoria or Kali offered her food, she had to force it down. She was in a state of limbo, living in a void where time was frozen, as were her feelings. She was in a state of nothingness.

It was not until the following morning that they finally received the all-clear. Kali called Kate to let her know and said she should continue to keep Buddy and Ginger with Carmen until they knew what the damage was.

"Ready?" Kali held her hand out to Jamie, who took it as she stood from the couch. In just a few days, she had become a shell of her former shelf. In the mirror, dark circles discolored the skin under her eyes, and her clothes hung a bit loosely on her frame. The depression she'd suffered as a teenager and young adult was nothing compared to the emptiness she now felt. She couldn't imagine what life without Ruth would be like, but she was about to find out.

"Ready," Jamie said as she walked out the door. They didn't know what they would be going home to, but more than that, they didn't know *whom* they would be going home to.

Victoria followed in silence until they stood facing the SUV. Fortunately, the insurance company had sent someone out to replace the windshield, but repairs to the body would take time.

"Let's go home," Kali said.

Victoria drove, Kali sat beside her, and Jamie took the back. As they merged onto the freeway going south, Jamie looked out the window, and some tears escaped down her cheek. Ruth had to be okay, she just had to, but Jamie closed her eyes and prepared herself for the worst. With the turn of a card, both the vineyard and her love could be gone. *Can a ghost die again?* And if so, would this be Ruth's transition? Would Jamie lose her to the one thing she said she always wanted…to leave the land? To finally rest in peace? Jamie selfishly didn't want Ruth to transition. Although deep down, she would feel happy that Ruth finally left the land, Jamie feared she would never recover from the loss. She dried her cheek as she inhaled a shaky breath. *Prepare yourself.*

Vic turned down the same road that had almost taken their lives. The cute little houses that once graced the hills were nothing but charred remains. Vegetation, black and dead, surrounded the pavement, and the trees that had tumbled to their death on the road had been cut into pieces and moved to the side. The fire was gone but would be forever felt in the scars of the survivors.

As they traveled deeper into the hills, a strange scene emerged. Sections of land and clusters of houses sat untouched next to scenes from a warzone. The fire had hopscotched its way indiscriminately, leaving both destruction and relief in its wake.

The initial reports claimed that five people had lost their lives, ten thousand acres were destroyed, and over a hundred structures had burned. Statistically not the worst wildfire California had seen, but the most personal for Jamie. The vineyard was where she'd not only found herself, she'd found love. It was the place where feeling the early morning breeze could transport her to the past, and a simple stroll through the grapevines could make a bad day turn good. This land held within it the magic of memories. This was the place and community that grounded her. And right now, her heart felt as destroyed as the land looked.

"Damn," Victoria said in a soft voice as they slowly made their way toward Chanadoah's Winery. Sections of that vast acreage were charred while others were left intact. Unfortunately, the iconic stone and wooden structure built generations ago that housed a tasting room, restaurant, and massive gift shop, had been burned to the ground. They drove by in silence, staring, transfixed between the memory of what had been and the reality of what was, the scene too eerie and upsetting to give a word or emotion to.

"Hopefully, they're all safe," Jamie whispered and made a mental note to check in with Mick to see how they could help. Fifteen minutes later, the SUV crested the hill that brought them to their property. "Holy shit," Vic said as she turned onto the gravel driveway. "Holy shit."

Miraculously, their vineyard stood almost entirely untouched. The entire southwest section was blacked and burned, but the fire had spared the majority of the land, house, and barn.

As Victoria drove up the driveway, Jamie's heart beat rapidly. She scanned the area for any sign of Ruth. *Where are you baby, where are you?*

"I don't see..." Kali began.

"There, stop the car. Stop the car!" Jamie flung open her door. Ruth was sitting on the front porch. She popped up and ran down the steps, disappeared, then materialized next to Jamie.

Jamie flung her arms around her. "I thought," Jamie mumbled as she kissed her. "I thought I would never see you again." She pulled away and cupped Ruth's face in her hands. Their relationship was going to come with a list of challenges, how could it not? But the love pouring out of Jamie's heart right then told her the beautiful soul who stood before her was worth it. "I love you, Ruth."

"I love you too."

Jamie pulled Ruth into a long, passionate kiss as desire surged through her body.

❖

"Come on," Kali said, "let's go check out the house and leave them alone. I really don't want to see ghost sex right now."

Victoria chuckled as she pulled the car close to the front porch and threw it in park. Kali hopped out and put her arm around Vic's waist and they walked up the steps and into the main room.

"It's nice to have a home to come back to," Kali said.

Vic leaned into her. "It sure is."

"Hmm, looks like the electricity is out," Kali said as she flipped the switch several times.

"I don't doubt it."

"I can't believe this old place is still standing." The charred houses of her neighbors flashed in Kali's head as she shuffled over to their sofa. They would lend a helping hand in whatever way they could as their neighbors returned to their properties and assessed damages. Kali felt a twinge of guilt as she wondered why their place had been spared and not others, but selfishly, that thought was soon replaced with a feeling of relief. Kali pulled her phone out of her back pocket and flopped down. "I'll call Kate and let her know we're home."

"Sounds good, babe," Victoria sat next to her, pulled off her shoes, and put her feet on the coffee table.

"Kate, you're not going to fucking believe it, but the house and barn are still standing and so is most of the vineyard. Call me."

The screen door opened, and Ruth and Jamie walked in.

"Ruth." Kali stood and hugged her as Jamie maneuvered past them and sat. "Good to see you again."

"You too, Kali." She sat next to Jamie.

"So, what happened after we left?" Victoria asked.

"It didn't take long for the fire to jump the road," Ruth said. "I grabbed the hose and continued spraying the house. I knew I couldn't save the vines, but maybe I could do a little something to help save a portion of the house. Then I noticed the orangish glow of the air was getting brighter and brighter. I looked over my shoulder, and the fire was already destroying the far corner of the vineyard and heading right toward the house."

Fear and sadness had washed over Ruth as she'd watched the flames devour the vines. She had been on this land over a hundred years, knew every inch of it intimately, and as much as she'd felt imprisoned by its boundaries, she'd ultimately developed a relationship with it. She'd talked to the plants, had touched the leaves, had enjoyed eating their fruit, and most importantly, she'd made memories with those who called it home. And for the first time since her death, Ruth had realized she no longer wanted to leave the land. She wanted to stay.

"Shit Ruth, weren't you scared?" Kali asked.

"I was. I knew deep down that when the flames reached me, they would take my soul. So I dropped the hose and walked up the porch and sat on Nora's bench. If I was finally going to leave, I wanted to do it while overlooking the vineyard."

It wasn't so much that Ruth had wanted her last vision to be the land itself, but more the people and memories that this land had brought her. She'd wanted to look out and see Nora and Kate dancing naked by the firepit, and Jamie walking around and singing. She had finally found the one who completed her. Jamie had made Ruth's journey through life and death worthwhile. Maybe this was the unfinished business Jamie had spoken of. Maybe she hadn't transitioned because she'd needed to find true love. And now she had. The thought saddened and excited her. If she would transition in the fire, she would do so knowing she'd finally found the one thing she had always sought. But leaving that behind had been a punch to the gut.

"But as I sat on the bench, watching the flames approach the firepit, something happened. A wind picked up, and the fire changed direction."

"Seriously?" Kali asked.

"Yeah. I couldn't believe it. When the sun came up, I got off the bench, and walked around. It was only then that I realized how close the fire came to destroying everything."

"Damn," Kali said as she started to stand. "I'm going to grab some wine. We need to make a toast."

❖

"I got it," Jamie said as she stood. "You stay there, I'll grab the bottle." Listening to how close Ruth had come to disappearing forever had caused a slight panic attack. Jamie needed to get off the couch and shake it out.

As she walked toward the kitchen, she glanced through the screen door at the vineyard and thought again about how lucky they were. The fire had spared many yet robbed many more. Jamie knew the area would slowly come together and rebuild itself, but the emotional toll would be huge. Structures could be rebuilt, but old vines and years of memories could never be replaced. They'd gotten lucky, very lucky. But as she headed into the kitchen, she wondered if luck really had nothing to do with it. Maybe Nora had been right. Maybe there really was a touch of magic on this land.

Epilogue

A year had passed since the fire, and unfortunately, Jamie had watched a handful of locals call it quits and leave for good, too devastated to rebuild. Insurance checks had been slow coming, and when they'd finally started to trickle in, everyone had complained that the amount wasn't enough to cover the full cost of the reconstruction. People had come together, as they always did in the wake of a disaster, and organized a variety of fundraisers, marathons, and concerts featuring local musicians, with all proceeds going to the fire relief fund. The area had been doing its best to heal. It would take time, and Jamie knew that for some, the healing would never come.

Chanadoah Winery was in the process of rebuilding. Mick boasted it would be bigger and better than before, and Jamie had no doubt that it would be spectacular. Several weeks ago, when their vineyard had been harvested, Jamie came up with the idea to sell their grapes to Mick at a discount price, with deferred payment until Chanadoah got their feet back on the ground. Fortunately, the vineyard's wedding business was going strong, and they'd all agreed that helping Mick out was the right thing to do.

They'd also expanded their family when the owner of an Appaloosa mare named C.W. lost everything in the fire and instead of rebuilding, had decided to move up to Portland to be closer to his son and grandkids. Since he was moving to a small townhouse, he'd asked Jamie if she wouldn't mind looking after the horse. Jamie asked Kate, who graciously adopted the mare, whom she nicknamed Dubbers.

Victoria had been promoted to public relations manager of Legacy's west coast division when Paige accepted an executive role at the company's office in Chicago. Ten months ago, Kali had asked Jamie and Kate if Vic could become a permanent resident at the vineyard, and Jamie couldn't have been happier. Recently, in a spontaneous move during a trip to a Las Vegas wine convention, Kali and Victoria had walked into a small white chapel on the strip and walked out married. For an extra hundred and fifty dollars, Kali had told Jamie, they could have had Elvis perform before the ceremony, but instead, they'd opted for a Cher impersonator.

Lately, Jamie noticed Victoria had been hit hard with kid fever, tearing up when any commercial with a cute kid came on and telling Kali how wonderful it would be if they had a child. Hoping to satisfy Victoria's hormonal surges, Jamie took Kali to the animal shelter after Kali confessed that she was not yet ready to take the parental plunge. Kali had adopted a high-maintenance, codependent, five-month-old terrier mix named Kona. For now, the bribe was working.

Kate and Linda had become close friends. What had started as a standing coffee date every Saturday turned into Linda becoming a fixture around the vineyard. When Jamie filled her in on Ruth, Linda had instantly embraced her. It seemed that the more loved ones people had lost in their life, the more open they were to the idea of a thin veil separating the known from the unknown. Jamie was happy Ruth gave Linda hope that her wife was out there somewhere, running around and having a good time.

When Jamie asked Kate if she and Linda ever crossed the physical line, Kate had told her Nora still held her heart, nothing was going to change that fact, and besides, menopause had cooled her physical urges years ago. Kate said that Linda provided a helping hand when the darkest moments came calling in the middle of the night, and memories haunted her mind.

Tonight, Jamie had invited Linda to the vineyard to perform a new song she'd written for a very special, private wedding.

"Okay, Linda," Kate said. "We're ready."

Linda started strumming the acoustic guitar as her alto voice filled the air. The full moon on the horizon and the little white lights that had become a permanent fixture glowed soft and beautiful, and as always, it gave the area that extra romantic touch. Kate stood under the floral archway and faced the only other people in attendance: Kali and Victoria.

"Ready, my love?" Jamie said as she reached out to Ruth.

"I am." Ruth smiled as she took Jamie's hand, turned and began walking. As always, she was dressed in her gray tweed pants, black suspenders, white shirt, and boots while Jamie wore a white, cotton-lace dress with a low-cut V-neck. Even though the wedding would never be registered in the eyes of any official agency, Jamie didn't care. They were about to be married in heart, mind, and soul, and that was all that mattered.

Kate stood under the archway and smiled as Jamie and Ruth faced each other.

"We are gathered here to witness the uniting of two beautiful souls, Jamie and Ruth. Two women who found each other under the most unusual circumstances, and who let love prevail. Who saw in each other the true meaning of love and not society's preconceived definition of what that love should look like. They are a testament to overcoming boundaries and stereotypes, and it is my privilege and honor to unite these souls in a bond that will forever bear witness to their love. Congratulations, Jamie and Ruth."

"Woo-hoo!" Kali jumped up and clapped in excitement as Ruth and Jamie kissed.

They walked to an eight-foot banquet table draped in white linen that sat in the middle of the staging area. In lieu of a wedding cake, Ruth had asked Kate to bake a batch of brownies, her new favorite. An assortment of food graced three chaffing dishes, and three bottles of *Four Friends* merlot sat waiting to be opened.

"To the brides," Kali announced as she popped a cork and poured.

"To the brides." Everyone raised their glasses and cheered.

An hour later, Kali jumped in their all-terrain golf cart and drove it over. Glow sticks were attached to the sides, a Just Married poster was taped to the back, and a few empty soup cans clanged on the ground behind it.

"All aboard," Kali said as she circled the brides. Ruth took the seat next to Kali, and Jamie got in the back. "I'm taking the brides to their honeymoon suite. Don't even think this party is over," Kali said to Vic, Kate, and Linda. "We will reconvene in the house when I return."

She floored it. They meandered to the far southeast corner where a rented RV had been parked. White lights were strung around the vehicle, and a sign on the door read, *Honeymoon suite, Do Not Disturb.*

Jamie laughed as Kali pulled in front of the RV. "I love it."

"I wanted to rent you an inflatable bounce house as a joke, but Kate threatened to cut off my pancake supply. She knows not what power she wields over me."

"Oh, I think she has a pretty good idea."

"Well...this is your stop." Kali parked, jumped out, and extended her hand to Ruth, then did the same for Jamie. "I shall leave you fair ladies to frolic while I go back to the party and partake in my own merriment. Farwell thee, fair maidens." She bowed, jumped back in the cart, and waved as she pulled away.

Ruth chuckled. "I think she's drunk."

"Nope, that's just Kali. Now, Mrs. Carr, what say ye and me head into the honeymoon suite and have some fun?"

"Why, Mrs. Carr, I thought you'd never ask." Ruth grabbed Jamie's hand, opened the door, and stepped in. The interior was covered in a variety of cute wedding decorations, a congratulations sign was draped from the ceiling, and small battery-operated candles flickered all over.

"What's this?" Ruth picked up a gift wrapped in silver paper.

"I don't know," Jamie said as she took it. A blue card taped to the paper read, *Have a vibratingly good time. Kali.* Jamie laughed and placed it down. "We'll save this one for later."

"Don't you want to see what it is?"

"Oh, I already know what it is, and tonight, I don't think we'll need it." She closed the distance between her and Ruth and kissed her hard. A moment later, her tongue took possession of Ruth's as the hunger to connect and feel her body took over. Jamie finally broke the embrace as she slowly removed Ruth's suspenders, then meticulously undid each button of her shirt and slowly peeled it away.

Ruth moaned as she started pulsing. "You're taking too much time."

"I'm allowing my mind to play with the fantasies of what I'm going to do to you."

"You're taking too long to figure that out."

"Trust me, baby, once we start, we're not coming up for air until morning," she whispered as she unbuttoned Ruth's pants and let them fall around her ankles. Ruth's underwear was soon to follow. Jamie kneeled and kissed around her belly button, then proceeded to go lower until she was right where she wanted to be. She ran a finger up and down Ruth's wetness as her tongue added extra sensation. Ruth gently pressed Jamie's head in closer...tighter...harder. "Bed...now," she moaned.

Jamie smiled as she looked up. She stood and led her to the back of the RV and the queen-size bed, but Ruth tripped and stumbled, almost causing them to fall. "Hmm, maybe I should have led with taking off your boots first. Sorry, babe."

Ruth plopped down in the cramped hallway and flung all her remaining clothes off as Jamie crawled to the middle of the bed and took a moment to admire Ruth's lean, muscular body. "Come here, baby," Jamie said.

Ruth slowly crawled on top of her, pinning her. She leaned down and kissed her hard.

"No fair," Jamie mumbled. "I thought I was the one in charge."

"Change of plans. Now take off that dress and let me feel you."

❖

"Yes, ma'am." Jamie smiled as she pulled her dress over her head in one swoop and squirmed out of everything else. Ruth took the moment to take in every inch, a view she would never tire of no matter how Jamie's body aged. "I think I'm liking this new you." Jamie moved to Ruth's mouth.

Ruth stuck her arm out and gently pushed Jamie back down. When they'd first gotten together, Ruth had been so unsure of herself, she'd let Jamie dictate the sex. Anything Jamie did, Ruth sent back. But bit by bit, Ruth had come into her own, and tonight, it was officially time to take control.

"Tonight," Ruth whispered, "I make love to you."

"But…"

Ruth placed a finger on Jamie's lips. "You can have me later. For now, I want you to lie there and let me take you."

"No arguments here."

Ruth gently placed Jamie's wrists above her head and kneeled over her body. She kissed Jamie hard. If Jamie tried to reach for her, she increased the pressure on Jamie's wrists, letting her know that *she* was in control right now.

Jamie responded by plunging her tongue deeper into Ruth's mouth as if telling her in every way that she was wet and more than willing to take whatever Ruth was offering. Ruth let the kiss linger, knowing she would never get tired of the way it felt. But eventually, desire won out, and she licked her way to Jamie's breasts. She gently sucked both nipples while still pinning Jamie to the bed.

Jamie moaned and arched her hips against Ruth's leg. Ruth playfully bit one nipple, causing Jamie to fall back to the bed.

"I'm in control," Ruth whispered as she loosened her grip and slowly moved her hands to Jamie's breasts. She licked her own finger and rubbed the wetness around Jamie's nipple, then slowly, ever so slowly, tickled it down.

Ruth felt Jamie's excitement the instant she reached between Jamie's legs. She was so excited herself that she wanted to penetrate Jamie now, but she stopped and reminded herself how much she was enjoying this ride. She ran her finger up and down Jamie's wetness until Jamie's moans grew deep. She increased her pace and applied some pressure. Jamie responded by tightening her thighs. Ruth took the cue, placed her tongue on Jamie's clit, and let it roll around and dance with the finger she held in place. Jamie moved her hips faster. This time, Ruth responded by pressing her lips down hard.

Jamie gently caressed her head as Ruth moved into her. Ruth increased the rhythm of her tongue and finger as she sensed Jamie was on the verge of coming.

"Yes, baby…yes."

When Jamie was about to come, Ruth took two fingers and penetrated her hard and fast. Jamie's orgasm was immediate and intense. Ruth could feel her throbbing as she continued to thrust. When she sensed Jamie coming down from her climax, Ruth slowed her fingers and gently pulled them out. She gave her one last kiss, then made her way up. She settled next to Jamie and placed one arm protectively around her.

"I love you, babe," Jamie whispered through an exhausted breath.

"I love you too," Ruth replied as she snuggled closer.

❖

The volume was low on the TV as Kate and Kali sat watching. An empty bottle of wine and three glasses sat next to a container of Kate's brownies. Victoria was asleep, her head on Kali's lap and her body curled around a snoring dog.

"Throw me another brownie." Kali fanned her fingers, ready for the catch.

Kate tossed it over to her.

"Do I smell sex?" Victoria lifted her head and mumbled without opening her eyes.

"No, baby, it's just one of Kate's brownies. Go back to sleep." Kali chuckled. "And here I thought I was the one with the addiction," she said as she took a bite.

"You two are made for each other." Kate leaned back and pressed herself in the cushion, twirling the silver wedding band on her finger. She had the ring for four months now, and she was still getting used to the way it felt.

"What are you thinking about?" Kali asked softly.

"Nora."

Kali nodded and turned her attention back to the TV and her brownie, no doubt giving Kate mental space. By the time the show's credits rolled, Kali was asleep, and Kate was well on her way. Through half-open eyes, she watched Buddy jump on the coffee table, swat the wine cork to the floor, leap down and carry it off. Her last thought before she succumbed to sleep was a mental note not to step in what was sure to be a slobbery mess of cork pieces scattered throughout the house when she got up to pee.

Kate dreamed of the moon continuing across the night sky, eventually tagging the sun so a bright orange glow kissed the vineyard good morning. Birds woke in beautiful song, and the slight breeze blew a fresh breath between the vines.

Life would continue to unfold on this land, and with it would come many more adventures that both embraced and broke the heart. But one thing was certain, magic would always be found on this land, to those that knew where to look.

About the Author

Toni Logan grew up in the Midwest but soon transplanted to the land of lizards and saguaro cactus. She loves hanging out with friends, eating insanely delicious vegan food, traveling to the beach (any beach), and hiking in the mountains. She shares her Arizona home with a terrier mix who thinks she's a queen and four rescued cats.

Books Available from Bold Strokes Books

A Far Better Thing by JD Wilburn. When needs of her family and wants of her heart clash, Cass Halliburton is faced with the ultimate sacrifice. (978-1-63555-834-0)

Body Language by Renee Roman. When Mika offers to provide Jen erotic tutoring, will sex drive them into a deeper relationship or tear them apart? (978-1-63555-800-5)

Carrie and Hope by Joy Argento. For Carrie and Hope loss brings them together but secrets and fear may tear them apart. (978-1-63555-827-2)

Death's Prelude by David S. Pederson. In this prequel to the Detective Heath Barrington Mystery series, Heath discovers that first love changes you forever and drives you to become the person you're destined to be. (978-1-63555-786-2)

Ice Queen by Gun Brooke. School counselor Aislin Kennedy wants to help standoffish CEO Susanna Durr and her troubled teenage daughter become closer—even if it means risking her own heart in the process. (978-1-63555-721-3)

Masquerade by Anne Shade. In 1925 Harlem, New York, a notorious gangster sets her sights on seducing Celine, and new lovers Dinah and Celine are forced to risk their hearts, and lives, for love. (978-1-63555-831-9)

Royal Family by Jenny Frame. Loss has defined both Clay's and Katya's lives, but guarding their hearts may prove to be the biggest heartbreak of all. (978-1-63555-745-9)

Share the Moon by Toni Logan. Three best friends, an inherited vineyard and a resident ghost come together for fun, romance and a touch of magic. (978-1-63555-844-9)

Spirit of the Law by Carsen Taite. Attorney Owen Lassiter will do almost anything to put a murderer behind bars, but can she get past her reluctance to rely on unconventional help from the alluring Summer Byrne and keep from falling in love in the process? (978-1-63555-766-4)

The Devil Incarnate by Ali Vali. Cain Casey has so much to live for, but enemies who lurk in the shadows threaten to unravel it all. (978-1-63555-534-9)

His Brother's Viscount by Stephanie Lake. Hector Somerville wants to rekindle his illicit love affair with Viscount Wentworth, but he must overcome one problem: Wentworth still loves Hector's brother. (978-1-63555-805-0)

Journey to Cash by Ashley Bartlett. Cash Braddock thought everything was great, but it looks like her history is about to become her right now. Which is a real bummer. (978-1-63555-464-9)

Liberty Bay by Karis Walsh. Wren Lindley's life is mired in tradition and untouched by trends until social media star Gina Strickland introduces an irresistible electricity into her off-the-grid world. (978-1-63555-816-6)

Scent by Kris Bryant. Nico Marshall has been burned by women in the past wanting her for her money. This time, she's determined to win Sophia Sweet over with her charm. (978-1-63555-780-0)

Shadows of Steel by Suzie Clarke. As their worlds collide and their choices come back to haunt them, Rachel and Claire must figure out how to stay together and most of all, stay alive. (978-1-63555-810-4)

The Clinch by Nicole Disney. Eden Bauer overcame a difficult past to become a world champion mixed martial artist, but now rising star and dreamy bad girl Brooklyn Shaw is a threat both to Eden's title and her heart. (978-1-63555-820-3)

The Last First Kiss by Julie Cannon. Kelly Newsome is so ready for a tropical island vacation, but she never expects to meet the woman who could give her her last first kiss. (978-1-63555-768-8)

The Mandolin Lunch by Missouri Vaun. Despite their immediate attraction, everything about Garet Allen says short-term, and Tess Hill refuses to consider anything less than forever. (978-1-63555-566-0)

Thor: Daughter of Asgard by Genevieve McCluer. When Hannah Olsen finds out she's the reincarnation of Thor, she's thrown into a world of magic and intrigue, unexpected attraction, and a mystery she's got to unravel. (978-1-63555-814-2)

Veterinary Technician by Nancy Wheelton. When a stable of horses is threatened Val and Ronnie must work together against the odds to save them, and maybe even themselves along the way. (978-1-63555-839-5)

16 Steps to Forever by Georgia Beers. Can Brooke Sullivan and Macy Carr find themselves by finding each other? (978-1-63555-762-6)

All I Want for Christmas by Georgia Beers, Maggie Cummings, Fiona Riley. The Christmas season sparks passion and love in these stories by award winning authors Georgia Beers, Maggie Cummings, and Fiona Riley. (978-1-63555-764-0)

From the Woods by Charlotte Greene. When Fiona goes backpacking in a protected wilderness, the last thing she expects is to be fighting for her life. (978-1-63555-793-0)

Heart of the Storm by Nicole Stiling. For Juliet Mitchell and Sienna Bennett a forbidden attraction definitely isn't worth upending the life they've worked so hard for. Is it? (978-1-63555-789-3)

If You Dare by Sandy Lowe. For Lauren West and Emma Prescott, following their passions is easy. Following their hearts, though? That's almost impossible. (978-1-63555-654-4)

Love Changes Everything by Jaime Maddox. For Samantha Brooks and Kirby Fielding, no matter how careful their plans, love will change everything. (978-1-63555-835-7)

Not This Time by MA Binfield. Flung back into each other's lives, can former bandmates Sophia and Madison have a second chance at romance? (978-1-63555-798-5)

The Dubious Gift of Dragon Blood by J. Marshall Freeman. One day Crispin is a lonely high school student—the next he is fighting a war in a land ruled by dragons, his otherworldly boyfriend at his side. (978-1-63555-725-1)

The Found Jar by Jaycie Morrison. Fear keeps Emily Harris trapped in her emotionally vacant life; can she find the courage to let Beck Reynolds guide her toward love? (978-1-63555-825-8)

Aurora by Emma L McGeown. After a traumatic accident, Elena Ricci is stricken with amnesia leaving her with no recollection of the last eight years, including her wife and son. (978-1-63555-824-1)

Avenging Avery by Sheri Lewis Wohl. Revenge against a vengeful vampire unites Isa Meyer and Jeni Denton, but it's love that heals them. (978-1-63555-622-3)

Bulletproof by Maggie Cummings. For Dylan Prescott and Briana Logan, the complicated NYC criminal justice system doesn't leave room for love, but where the heart is concerned, no one is bulletproof. (978-1-63555-771-8)

Her Lady to Love by Jane Walsh. A shy wallflower joins forces with the most popular woman in Regency London on a quest to catch a husband, only to discover a wild passion for each other that far eclipses their interest for the Marriage Mart. (978-1-63555-809-8)

No Regrets by Joy Argento. For Jodi and Beth, the possibility of losing their future will force them to decide what is really important. (978-1-63555-751-0)

The Holiday Treatment by Elle Spencer. Who doesn't want a gay Christmas movie? Holly Hudson asks herself that question and discovers that happy endings aren't only for the movies. (978-1-63555-660-5)

Too Good to be True by Leigh Hays. Can the promise of love survive the realities of life for Madison and Jen, or is it too good to be true? (978-1-63555-715-2)

Treacherous Seas by Radclyffe. When the choice comes down to the lives of her officers against the promise she made to her wife, Reese Conlon puts everything she cares about on the line. (978-1-63555-778-7)

Two to Tangle by Melissa Brayden. Ryan Jacks has been a player all her life, but the new chef at Tangle Valley Vineyard changes everything. If only she wasn't off the menu. (978-1-63555-747-3)

When Sparks Fly by Annie McDonald. Will the devastating incident that first brought Dr. Daniella Waveny and hockey coach Luca McCaffrey together on frozen ice now force them apart, or will their secrets and fears thaw enough for them to create sparks? (978-1-63555-782-4)

Best Practice by Carsen Taite. When attorney Grace Maldonado agrees to mentor her best friend's little sister, she's prepared to confront Perry's rebellious nature, but she isn't prepared to fall in love. Legal Affairs: one law firm, three best friends, three chances to fall in love. (978-1-63555-361-1)

Home by Kris Bryant. Natalie and Sarah discover that anything is possible when love takes the long way home. (978-1-63555-853-1)

Keeper by Sydney Quinne. With a new charge under her reluctant wing—feisty, highly intelligent math wizard Isabelle Templeton—Keeper Andy Bouchard has to prevent a murder or die trying. (978-1-63555-852-4)

One More Chance by Ali Vali. Harry Basantes planned a future with Desi Thompson until the day Desi disappeared without a word, only to walk back into her life sixteen years later. (978-1-63555-536-3)

Renegade's War by Gun Brooke. Freedom fighter Aurelia DeCallum regrets saving the woman called Blue. She fears it will jeopardize her mission, and secretly, Blue might end up breaking Aurelia's heart. (978-1-63555-484-7)

The Other Women by Erin Zak. What happens in Vegas should stay in Vegas, but what do you do when the love you find in Vegas changes your life forever? (978-1-63555-741-1)

The Sea Within by Missouri Vaun. Time is running out for Dr. Elle Graham to convince Captain Jackson Drake that the only thing that can save future Earth resides in the past, and rescue her broken heart in the process. (978-1-63555-568-4)

To Sleep With Reindeer by Justine Saracen. In Norway under Nazi occupation, Maarit, an Indigenous woman; and Kirsten, a Norwegian resister, join forces to stop the development of an atomic weapon. (978-1-63555-735-0)

Twice Shy by Aurora Rey. Having an ex with benefits isn't all it's cracked up to be. Will Amanda Russo learn that lesson in time to take a chance on love with Quinn Sullivan? (978-1-63555-737-4)

Z-Town by Eden Darry. Forced to work together to stay alive, Meg and Lane must find the centuries-old treasure before the zombies find them first. (978-1-63555-743-5)